EVIE MITCHELL

Runner

Book 1 | Nameless Souls MC

First edition

ISBN: 978-0-6489687-7-1

Editing by Nicole Wilson, Evermore Editing
Cover art by Tash Drake, Outlined with Love Designs

This book was professionally typeset on Reedsy.
Find out more at reedsy.com

Books by Evie Mitchell

Nameless Souls MC Series
Runner
Wrath
Ghost

Elliot Security Series
Rough Edge
Bleeding Edge
Knife Edge

Capricorn Cove Series
Thunder Thighs
Double the D
Muffin Top
The Mrs. Clause
Beach Party
New Year Knew You
The Shake-Up
Double Breasted
As You Wish
You Sleigh Me
Resolution Revolution
Meat Load
Trunk Junk

Archer Sibling Series
Just Joshing
Thor's Shipbuilding Series
Clean Sweep
The X-List
Reality Check
The Christmas Contract

Other Books
Reign
Puppy Love

Dedication

To you, Greedy Reader.
For supporting me through the pandemic and allowing me to pen
this nonsense.

And to my husband, thank you for being my rock.
When life gives us lemons you don't make lemonade, you make
freaking lemon meringue pie. It's why I have thunder thighs. Love
you.

Connect with Evie Mitchell

Newsletter
Bookbub
Amazon
Facebook
Greedy Readers Book Club
Instagram
Goodreads

Runner

Ellie

The virus ravaged the world, plunging us into darkness. It was in the darkness that nightmares became reality.

And it was in the shadows that I met him—Runner. He promised me protection in exchange for one thing—my surrender.

Runner

She was salvation. Bringing us hope when all was lost.

I'd fight for her. For our life together. But in the after nothing is guaranteed.

When the world ended, we began. But would we have a future?

Trigger warning: This is a darker book than my other series and contains some violence and references to abuse. A happily ever after is still guaranteed, but this is a gritty series so proceeded with caution.

Prologue

Day 402 – Post the Dark

I know Audrey said to treat this as a written history of what happened after the world went dark but these entries feel more like a diary. So here goes.

Dear Diary,

The thing I wasn't expecting when the world ended is that it's a lot of anxiety mixed with boredom mixed with uncertainty mixed with the occasional rapid moment of action. Turns out Armageddon doesn't happen overnight. This was a long, slow death of all we had known.

When the virus came and people became sick, the governments started closing borders and ordering citizens home. They did their best to contain it, and some countries even succeeded—though from reports we hear occasionally, it looks like they're struggling once more.

I'm not an idiot. When the world started going to shit, I did what any sensible person does, I found like-minded people and we formulated a plan. The plan was both electronic and in hard copy (should the electrical grid fail), colour-coded, and contained multiple end-case scenario options built upon the

1

best available data.

We tracked the data, diligently inputting information into our systems, checking and rechecking the options. Consistently, the most plausible scenario was a full disintegration of governmental order.

St. Mary Women's College sat proudly by the sea. Located in a small town, hours away from the closest cities, we had a longer window of time to consider what came next. And we decided that while our classmates rushed to return home, we would recruit a band of women who had the skills to handle whatever our future might be.

As the world ended, and the stories of death and destruction spread, it didn't take us long to find women to recruit. We pooled resources, found friends who had family with the skills and knowledge we needed, and we ran scenario after scenario—all of which said that we were best placed to stay where we were.

So, we did. When the University shut its doors and ordered students home, we bunkered down fortifying our position.

Ultimately there were thirteen of us—lucky or not we weren't yet sure. Most came from the University, but some were siblings who had skills we needed. We'd been clear from the start—no men or children. When we added them to the scenario things got... messy.

In the end, there's my older sister, Blair, who'd returned to the College for a semester to research a new technique to treat the virus. Aella, in her final year of nursing, was only three weeks shy of graduating. Her sister, Yana, had been a professional chef and had experience in food preservation. Lilith was completing her PhD in electrical engineering, while Kate studied botany.

The Berger sisters are country girls, Ruby and Beth were at the College studying agriculture and animal science respectively, while their older sister, Jo, is a mechanic who's come to see out the after with us.

We also have Jules, our hydrologist, Audrey is a network engineer and our numbers girl, and me, Ellison, the biochemist of the group.

Our final two are Charlotte, or Lottie as she prefers to be known, who is our veterinarian, and her sister, Ava, a soldier. Ava had been on medical leave when shit started to get real—lucky for her. She'd arrived packing some truly frightening arsenal and a look in her eye that said she wasn't afraid to use it.

When the world finally lost its collective mind, and the shooting and rioting spread from the major cities to small towns like ours, we'd bunkered down at the College, Ava securing the perimeter, the rest of us working on our respective fields to secure our survival.

And we'd somehow ended up living like that for four hundred and one days. Turns out, when the world goes to shit, people forget about schools, universities, and the like. They search factories, businesses, stores, and homes looking for food and equipment but forget all about colleges.

The few that did wander into our little bubble were quickly dealt with by Ava. Most left. One or two I still don't know what happened to—and to be honest, I never want to know.

Our little group functioned well. Between us, we've been attempting to produce bioethanol, and have built solar and wind options to generate power. We've planted vegetables and constructed greenhouses. We even have a 3D printer which allows us to print extra weaponry for Ava.

We share knowledge and learned self-defense. Kate taught us about edible and poisonous plants. Jules showed us how to test water and design hydroponic set-ups. Lilith taught us how to generate electricity from wind. Everyone brought something to the table.

Life was good.

Until last night. Until the night of The Purge.

Chapter One

Ellie

"What other choice do we have?" Blair asked the round table. We were missing two of our close-knit family group—grief, worry, anxiety, anger etched on the faces and burned into the souls of everyone in the room.

"Do we think they'll be back?" Yana asked the question we were all avoiding, her eyes on the cameras monitoring the boundaries of the University.

"They know there are women here. They'll definitely come back." Jo shook her head. "We're trained, but we're outnumbered."

"Did you see their women?" Beth, the youngest of our party, asked in a whisper. "They looked…"

"Dead," Jo said with a nod. "Chained up and used for nothing but sex."

When we'd killed some of their party, the women had scattered, running naked into the dark. Lilith and Jules had followed. We'd tried to find them but had lost them in the bush surrounding the College when The Purge had mounted another attack forcing us back.

We'd survived, mainly thanks to Ava. But we didn't know if Jules and Lilith were alive or taken.

"We're idiots if we stay here another night," Jo muttered.

"But where would we go?" Jules asked.

We all fell silent. *Isn't that the million-dollar question?*

Since the world as we knew it had officially ended some nine months before, we'd built our own town. Living out of our abandoned University, the thirteen of us had felt safe. Secure. Insulated from the horrors of the outside world. Or as safe and secure as you could be when you were living in the aftermath of an apocalypse.

Until The Purge.

Audrey shoved her glasses up her nose, blinking at the screen of the laptop in her hands. "I've run the scenarios. Based on their losses and what we could find out from the one guy Ava... Ava...." She swallowed, forging forward. "We have three days to either leave the College or find assistance to fortify our defenses." She looked up, frown lines creasing her brow. "Do we have anyone who could help us?"

"The guy said they had over forty people, right?" I asked, looking to Ava.

"Yeah, though the numbers seemed pretty fluid. The main currency is women, food, and guns. We're sitting ducks," Ava said. She was sprawled on her side in a bed by the table, her face pale, sweat-dampened her brow. She'd taken a knife to her side but kept fighting, keeping us safe and capturing one of them. She'd taken him to the basement and she'd remained in there for hours, emerging much later to hand over her intel. She'd let Blair patch her up, but refused to remain in the infirmary while we discussed options.

"Fuck," Jo barked, pushing to her feet, and beginning to pace.

"We have to leave. Got no other choice."

"I... I m-m-might have an idea," Kate whispered, her hand rising ever so slightly. She only ever stuttered under extreme anxiety or when scared.

All eyes went to her and she blushed, looking down at the table.

"Go on," I encouraged, knowing Kate shied easily.

"M-my father," she stuttered, staring at the table.

"One man isn't gonna fix this, babe."

"Shh," I hushed Jo, then looked back at Kate. "Keep going."

"H-h-h-he is th-th-the P-P-President of the Nameless Souls m-m-motorcycle club."

"A gang?" Jo said, her eyes narrowing. "Your daddy is a member of a gang?"

"It's a c-club but, yeah, he r-r-runs it."

There was a beat of silence as we processed this news. *How did we not know this?*

"They're an outlaw gang," Ava murmured, grimacing when she shifted. "If your dad is part of this club, why are you here? Why not throw your lot in with them?"

Kate flushed and looked away, biting her lip.

"Kate?" I asked softly.

"A w-w-woman in the club n-n-n-needs a man. You're not you, you're p-p-p-property."

"Property?" Jo asked.

Kate nodded.

"I've read about this," Blair sighed, rubbing her temples. "They don't have female bikers. They have two types of women—club sluts or old ladies."

"What's the difference?"

"The old ladies are claimed, they call them property. Like

7

wives so they're afforded some modicum of respect. The sluts, not so much."

We all grimaced.

Kate looked down, rubbing the tabletop with shaky hands.

"What are they going to want if we ask them for help?" Ava asked.

Kate shrugged, still looking down. "M-m-maybe food. Definitely sex."

"Fuck," Ava muttered.

An idea tickled the back of my mind. "What about fuel?"

Kate cocked her head in question.

"The bioethanol and biodiesels we're using to run the vehicles. Could we trade that? I'm still fine-tuning, it's taken me a while to work out how to scale because we don't have all the parts or ingredients but we have enough that I could offer them a sample. If it worked, maybe that could be our in. Do you think they'd go for a trade? Fuel and help with, I don't know, energy? Water? Whatever they need in exchange for protection."

The women looked excited but Kate shook her head. "They'd just t-t-take it anyway."

"But we could try," I said, unwilling to just give up. "Do we have any other choice?"

"Let's put it to a vote," Jo ordered, looking around the table. "Those in favour of leaving."

Two hands.

"Those in favour of approaching the bikers?"

Eight hands went up.

"Kate, you didn't vote," Jo admonished.

She kept stroking the grain of the wooden table, her eyes fixed on her hands, a single tear slipping down her cheek. "I-I-

I'll do w-w-whatever you agree to."

"Then we're settled. We'll approach the bikers."

Ava blew out a breath. "I can't go. Not like this, at least not today. And we need to shore up shit in case the biker stuff doesn't pan out. Need to get our stuff ready to evac."

"I'll go," I volunteered. "Kate will need to come as well. Anyone else?"

"Jo," Ava ordered. "And Audrey."

We all blinked in surprise.

"Me?" Audrey asked, shoving her glasses up her nose. "But… why?"

" I trust you to strategize if things go south." She nodded at Jo. "Jo can talk bikes, try and sell our skills. Ellie has the knowledge to produce biofuel, something they'll likely want with fuel supplies getting low. And Kate will get us an audience with the President."

"Okay," I muttered, pushing to my feet. "Guess we better get our stuff together."

"We'll leave within the hour," Jo ordered. "I'm not risking us for longer than necessary."

We began to disband, people leaving and Blair pushing Ava's bed out the door. Only Kate remained sitting, her gaze fixed on the table.

"Kate?"

She didn't respond.

"Is there something you're not telling us?"

She raised one shoulder then dropped it.

Fear prickled my spine.

"Is it bad?"

"Not for you."

I dropped back into my seat, leaning towards her, trying to

catch her eye.

"Tell me."

She shook her head, her eyes filled with fear.

"Please?"

"Y-y-you'll see," she whispered.

Chapter Two

Ellie

We took one of the SUVs, the back loaded with bioethanol and food. Jo had a shotgun lying across her lap, her gaze on the trees outside as Kate drove through the deserted streets out to the country.

The local town had been abandoned months ago. We occasionally ventured out, looking for extra items to supplement our stores or fulfil a need. The small populace that had remained in the area had left when winter took hold and food became scarce. We'd weathered the winter months well, Kate and Ruby tending to our greenhouses and slaughtering the occasional animal for protein. Spring was now here, but the town remained deserted.

"The Purge came from the north," Jo muttered, as if to reassure herself.

The Purge. A group that'd formed following society's downfall. Frat boys and mean men who'd hidden behind suits and uniforms in the before. Their true colours had emerged in the after as they viewed what remained as an anarchist dream; women, riches, and life no more than commodities they were

11

willing to trade. The group that had reached us were scouts; those sent ahead to search for plundering opportunities.

Please let these bikers agree to help us... and for minimal cost.

We travelled for three hours before Kate finally turned off, following a road that only she seemed to know. I'd spent the entire journey fisting my weapon petrified that militia, The Purge, or some idiot with a gun would jump out, taking us by surprise.

The actual journey was much more boring.

"Are you sure this is right?" Jo asked, her foot tapping nervously as we bounced along the track.

"It's just over the hill," Kate said nodding towards a large hill backlit by the moon in the distance.

We drove in silence along the dirt road, the trail barely visible through the brush. I'd have assumed this were an animal trail if Kate hadn't turned off, looking increasingly determined and fearful the closer we got to the Club House.

"What if they're not here?" Audrey asked, her hands twitching as if she wished for an electronic to play with. "What if they've left?"

"Then we have a new base of operations," Jo replied easily. She waved a hand at the brush outside. "No one would find us here."

That was the point, I suspected. Anyone who stumbled across the MC would likely stumble no further.

My stomach churned, a lump of anxious nerves writhing inside me.

This has to work.

Kate continued to bump us along the track and over the hill, a thick ring of trees grew on the other side. She drove directly toward two trees, the SUV following the faint trail through the gap between them.

"I thought you said—" Jo broke off as we exited the tree line and entered a clearing. On the far side sat an intimidating building. A tall chain-link fence surrounded the property, barbed wire twisted in circles at the top. Behind the chain-link was another wall, this one thick brick and topped with razor wire. The fences blocked everything from view but for the top of one building. From this distance it looked like the top of a castle, a battlement complete with a flag.

"They really want to keep people out," Audrey muttered.

Or in.

I chose not to voice that thought.

Kate slowed the SUV to a crawl and flashed her lights. There was a pause as the SUV continued at a snail's pace then a returning three flashes came from a position close to the ground.

"What was that?" Jo asked, her hands clenching on the rifle.

"Approval," Kate said, steering us in the direction of where the light had come from. Two men stood on the outside of the fence, their bodies covered in protective gear, large guns pointed straight at us.

Kate pulled to a stop and wound the window down, calling, "It's K-K-K-Kate R-R-R-Redwin. I'm here to see the Prez."

"Kate!" One of the men exclaimed, moving to her window. He held up a flashlight, shining it in the vehicle. "Well, fuck me dead. Little Katie! Where you been, girly? Your daddy's been frantic."

"C-can we go in?" she asked, lifting her hand to shield her eyes from the light.

"Who you got with you?"

"F-friends."

13

"Hot ones," came the reply from the other side of the car. "Women."

"Fresh meat?" the original guy asked Kate. She shook her head.

"Friends."

"Don't mean they aren't interested in becoming fresh meat." The second guy said, dropping a hand to clasp at his junk. "You ladies want this? I can protect you real nice."

In the dim light I could make out the patches on his vest, one read *prospect*, the other *Gears*.

"We're good," Jo drawled dryly. "But thank you for the magnificent offer."

He grinned, unperturbed. "I call dibs on this one. She's gonna be fun."

"*She* is right here and can hear you. And *she* said she wasn't interested."

He shook his head. "Let 'em through, Fish. The Prez will wanna see this."

The first man stepped back and waved us through. The gate opened and Kate navigated us down a dirt and gravel drive into the heart of the compound.

"Was that guy's name really Fish?" Audrey asked, twisting to look back at the two men.

"Nickname," Kate answered, her hands white knuckling the steering wheel.

"What kind of nickname is Fish?"

Kate didn't answer and Audrey slowly turned back around, watching as we passed through the second gate.

The compound was much larger than I anticipated. A giant building took up the space in front of us, behind it sat a cluster of buildings, their purpose unclear. The space was so big I couldn't see either end of the lot.

"What is this place?" Jo muttered as Kate pulled to a stop before the main building.

"Ex-army c-c-c-compound. The big b-b-building is the C-C-Club House. The others are m-m-mess halls or sleeping q-q-quarters or storage," Kate replied, undoing her seat belt, and exiting the car. "B-b-be careful, stay c-c-close."

We followed her, the cool air dancing along our skin.

"Be careful, they're watching," Audrey breathed in my ear nodding at the lights. I observed them, noting that parts of the yard were lit, the lights directed purposefully at the entrance, as if to blind anyone seeking to enter. It made it difficult to see through to the shadows, the only thing I could get a sense of was movement.

The door to the main compound opened and a man strode out, arms thrown open in welcome.

"Katie-girl! Ye've returned to your pa!"

I saw Kate tense then forcibly relax; a tight smile pasted on her face. "Pa," she greeted walking into his arms, returning his hug. He pressed kisses to her head, shaking her from side to side.

"Me wee darling has returned to the fold," he boomed, his voice carrying across the yard. "And she's brought friends." He turned Kate, pulling her into his side and walking her across to where we stood. Men, big, muscular, scary-looking men with weapons, and suspicious, hungry eyes emerged from the darkness, weapons trained on us.

One man caught my eye. Even in the dark he looked tan; his long, lean but muscular body reminded me of MMA fighters from the before. He met my gaze, awareness flaring between us, his gaze hungry as he dropped his eyes, looking me over from top to toe.

I shivered, tearing my eyes away to refocus on Jo and the President.

"Great welcome party you got here," Jo said, palming her own rifle and baring her teeth at the gathering men.

"Ye want to pop that away, love?" The President asked her, his voice bland but his face hard. "Me men don't take kindly to strangers bringing guns in here."

Jo raised an eyebrow. "And I don't take kindly to men I don't know pointing weapons at me."

I watched, my heart hammering through my chest as the President considered her.

"Alright boy-o's, let's show the ladies some hospitality."

Weapons were holstered, but Jo hesitated for a moment then lifted the rifle, laying it on her shoulder.

"Obliged," she said, giving him a nod.

The President grinned, his salt-and-pepper beard baring teeth. "I like a feisty woman." He gave Kate a little shake. "Not like me little Katie here. Meek as a church mouse, aren't ye, me darling?"

She dropped her head, curling in on herself.

I gritted my teeth, uncomfortable with both Kate's reaction and the surrounding men.

"Come, we'll break bread and talk." He looked from Audrey to Jo and then rested on me. "I don't imagine you're here to simply visit."

We followed him into the compound, the men surrounding us. The hair on the back of my neck prickled, my gut churning.

Something wasn't right.

We were led through an entry into the main parlour. Stocked with a bar, pool table, and plenty of couches, tables, and chairs. Women in low cut tops, tight jeans, and heavy make-up watched us with narrowed eyes as we walked through, following Kate and the President to a backroom. The sign on the door read *Church*.

Audrey drifted closer, her hands low but close enough to sign, *I don't like this.*

Agreed, I signed back.

Ava had taught us. She'd explained that sometimes we might need alternate ways to communicate and while she had taught us military signs for battle, she'd also insisted we learn sign language in case we were captured and needed to plan an escape.

I silently thanked God for the day Ava had arrived in our little group.

"Take a seat," the President ordered, sweeping a hand to encompass the room. The room was windowless but held two doors. One at the front where we entered, and another at the rear. A large rectangular table dominated the space, surrounded by twenty seats, an ornate chandelier hung above it, the dim lights casting an ominous glow around the room.

The President sat at the head, the rest of the men moving to take up seats with engravings like *Vice President* or *Warlord* on the back. On the walls hung photos of various bikes, names inscribed below. Based on the number I assumed they were memorials to deceased club members.

I glanced at Jo then settled at the table, taking a seat that wasn't marked. She paused for a moment then sat beside me, placing the rifle on the table in front of her. Audrey and Kate took two seats across from us. The rest of the men moved around, taking any spare seats, or leaning casually against the walls.

The seat at the far end of the table remained empty, *Old Timer* was burnt into the wood. I assumed that was meaningful but didn't think this was the moment to ask.

The man who'd watched me earlier had taken an assigned seat, though I couldn't see the title on his chair. He watched me with an intensity I found at once thrilling and terrifying.

The knife in my boot and the pistol in the back of my jeans itched, almost insisting I pull them free. I stayed in place, waiting, attempting not to draw further attention to myself.

The President cracked a gavel, calling the meeting to order. "I'm Gus, but you can call me President." He didn't introduce his men.

I took a moment to study Kate's father. They shared piercing blue eyes, the colour of deep oceans, beautiful and startling. They also shared dark, long lashes and a dimple on their right cheek. But that's where the similarities ended.

Gus was dark and weathered, his skin carved by years of sun. He was full chested and beer-bellied. He emitted an air that said, come at me. A confidence that promised those looking for retribution.

Kate was a curvy, stunning woman. Strawberry-blonde hair, average height, the thick full body of pin-ups from a bygone era. She had an economy of movement that said she loved the outdoors, loved to move, loved to dance. She moved like poetry, sensual and flowing, unconsciously beautiful and alluring.

Today, with her hunched shoulders and averted eyes, she moved like a woman hoping to avoid notice.

"I'm Jo, this is Audrey and Ellison," Jo introduced with a sweep of her arm. "We're here with a proposition."

Kate sat meekly across the table, looking for all the world like a dutiful daughter. But her hands were clenched and I could see the whites of her knuckles.

"So ye've not come to return my daughter to me?" Gus asked.

"Kate's her own person. You don't return someone to another," Audrey replied. She tilted her head to one side, glasses sliding down her nose. Absently, she pushed them back up. "And it's not as if you came looking for her."

Gus raised an eyebrow, looking down at his daughter.

"What lies have ye been spreading, love? Are ye one to believe this feminist nonsense?"

I watched as Kate struggled to lift her head, her eyes flashing even as the colour ebbed from her face. "Th-th-they're my friends, P-P-Pa. And we've survived this long without a m-m-man."

"But ye're here, aren't ye?" he scoffed.

"To trade," Jo said firmly, leaning forward. "We have something you want."

"We've gash enough around this place," Gus dismissed with a wave of his hand.

"Gash?" I asked.

"W-women," Kate answered for her father.

We were all silent for a moment while the men around the table chuckled.

"We've got fuel," I finally said, deciding to take over the negotiation. All heads twisted; amusement wiped from their faces.

"Fuel?" Gus asked, a hand lifting to stroke his beard. "And pray, how did ye come by such a bounty?"

"I made it."

There was a beat of silence before Gus leaned forward, pressing a hand to the table. "Ye did what now?"

I swallowed, deeply aware of the way in which the men at

19

the table watched me—as if I were a mouse and them the cats ready to pounce.

"I'm a biochemist, or at least, I was. My specialty was biofuels. Renewables. Using different products to create viable alternatives. I'd nearly landed on a new formula before everything went... well, bad. Anyways, I've spent the last few months working to perfect some options and we've done tests. The bioethanol I've created works like petroleum. I haven't been able to make a diesel alternative yet that can scale, the composition is difficult and I just don't have many available resources but with time and—"

Jo interrupted me, "What Ellie is trying to say, is that we've tested it. It works. And I know for a fact you're going to want it."

"A fact?" Gus asked, his tone deceptively mild.

"You got bikes and cars parked out front. The truck has cobwebs and long grass under it. The bikes are showing signs of sun wear. I'm gonna hazard a guess that you, like everyone else in this God forsaken country, are starting to find your stores running low."

Silence dominated the room.

"Ellie's fuel works. I'm a mechanic by trade. The SUV we drove here, it's been using her fuel for two months, no problems. You got a choice, you help us, we'll supply you with the fuel."

"And if we don't?"

"We'll walk out of here and you can go back to scavenging."

Gus rubbed his chin, as if considering Jo's offer.

"A man don't take too kindly to ultimatums being tossed his way in his own house."

"I don't take too kindly to our lives being threatened, so sorry if I'm a little impatient."

Gus's gaze sharpened. "Threatened?"

"The Purge found our safe house. You heard of them?"

Behind me someone swore, one of the guys turned to the side and spat on the floor.

"We're aware of that lot," Gus confirmed. He looked over at Kate. "Ye have a run-in with them lot?"

"S-s-scouts. We know more are c-c-coming."

"Ye get a number?"

"Around forty," Jo answered. "We either need to move or we need more numbers to help protect us."

Gus tapped a finger on the table. "Ye're asking a lot of me. The Purge is well armed. Why not just relocate ye four here?"

We were silent a beat too long. Gus sucked in a breath. "There's more of ye."

We didn't reply but our silence said everything.

"Women?" he asked, leaning forward, gaze sharp.

"Yes," Jo finally answered, making the decision.

"Men?"

"No."

"Bairns?"

"No, no children."

"Just women?"

"Yes."

There were murmurings around the table, men looking at us with new interest.

"How many?"

"You don't need to know that."

"How many!?" Gus slammed his fist on the table, causing us to jump.

Jo hesitated then gave in. "We number eleven now."

I sent up a silent prayer for Lilith and Jules, hoping they were simply lost rather than taken.

"Eleven women," a man breathed behind me.

There was an undercurrent here, something I wasn't aware of. My neck prickled and I glanced up the table, finding the man's gaze directly on me again. He wore his vest—no, his kutte, Kate had called it—well. The leather cut off at the shoulders, revealing a black shirt and thick, muscular biceps. He needed a shave and a haircut but he was still easily the most beautiful man I'd ever seen.

I looked away, a flush heating my cheeks.

"How long have ye been hiding?"

"Since before."

There were murmurs, the men shifting at our pronouncement.

Audrey looked around, frowning. "What are we missing?"

"Have ye all been vaccinated?"

"We were, in the before." Jo confirmed. "Obviously not against this new shit, but the regular stuff? Like polio and hepatitis, yeah."

The men's murmurs grew, a ripple of excitement flowing across the room.

I didn't like it. Not one bit.

"What is happening?" Audrey demanded. "What is this about?"

Her outburst silenced the table.

"The virus mutated, love. Women, they're afflicted. Ye a commodity now. There's so few of ye left that eleven is a boon the likes my men rarely see."

Bile burned the back of my throat.

A boon. A fucking commodity. These men aren't any better than

The Purge.

"Ye not safe wherever ye've been living, my loves. If they know about ye, they'll be back to take ye."

Jo stood abruptly, pushing back from the table to pace. Men parted for her, their faces carved in stone.

"Mutated how?"

A man from the side of the room answered. "They're carriers of what we're calling the Bastard strain. Aggressive, deadly. It turns your blood to filth, either destroying you from the inside or mutating your own genes to become a carrier."

"God," Audrey muttered, "this is sounding more and more like a zombie apocalypse every day."

No one laughed.

"I'll not bring my sisters here to be raped," Jo gritted out. "Or to be used as if we're nothing but baby makers. We're intelligent, educated. We've survived this long without you. We can do it again. We don't need you. You need us."

Audrey's eyes were closed, her lips moving silently. I bit my lip, knowing she was playing the possible scenarios, running the numbers.

"If I give ye my word, if I place me patch on each of ye, will ye come?"

"But," I protested, "our farm, our animals, what about our lab?"

"The l-l-library," Kate whispered, her eyes wide. "We need k-k-knowledge to survive."

Her father made a dismissive sound in his throat. "Ye and ye bloody books."

"They're not bloody anything," Kate protested, suddenly bold. "They've s-s-saved us. Without the knowledge in them we wouldn't have k-k-known how to print the rifles or build bullets or greenh-h-houses or—"

Gus interrupted his daughter with a wave. "Fine, if ye move in, I promise to transport ye things here." His gaze cut to Jo. "Does that satisfy ye?"

Jo crossed her arms, tapping one foot. "That depends on Audrey."

Everyone looked to the small, dark haired woman. She kept her eyes closed for another long few minutes before blinking them open and looking at Jo. "Accept the offer."

The tension in the room eased.

"Are you sure?" Jo demanded.

"If what they're saying is true, then we have bigger issues and the numbers are against us."

"What's bigger than The Purge?"

"The virus," Audrey whispered, sweeping her hands out to encompass the room. "We'll need to reproduce at some stage. And when that happens our children may be susceptible to common viruses if we don't have access on an ongoing basis to facilities to reproduce common vaccines. If Blair's research is to continue then we need to be somewhere that we can study the virus over time, not have to pick up and run regularly." She nodded at the room at large. "These men give us an eighty-three percent chance at finding, if not a cure, then at least a viable vaccine."

"And if we stay?"

"Between The Purge, the possible new infection strain, potential issues with interbreeding of our live stock in the next few years, not to mention increased militia groups, I give us a thirteen percent chance of survival."

"Don't forget the cannibals," the man next to me muttered.

Cannibals? What the fuck?

Jo ran a hand through her short hair, leaving it standing on end. Around her, the men watched as she made her decision.

"I need a guarantee you won't harm us. That your men won't force my women to do something they don't want to."

Gus rubbed his chin as he considered Jo. "What about we grant ye a boon?"

Jo blinked. "Excuse me?"

"We'll consider ye property, old ladies. We respect property. My men won't fuck with another man's toy—that right boys?"

The gathered men affirmed his declaration.

"You want us to choose a protector? Someone to fuck and suck without even knowing them?" Jo demanded.

"We'll return the favour," one of the men shouted from the side, setting off scattered laughter.

Jo shook her head. "Not gonna happen."

"Ye don't have to choose a man," Gus rolled his eyes. "Ye dramatics are doing me fucking head in." He leaned forward. "I'm granting ye the same rights as an old lady would have. Without the need for a man."

Audrey tipped her head to the side. "But just say we want a man, exactly how many of you are there?"

There were grins at her question.

I sunk down in my chair, face heating. Audrey had no filter. "Over fifty."

"And how many are married?"

"Ye mean, how many have old ladies?"

"Sure, whatever." Audrey waved a dismissive hand.

"Ah, about half."

Twenty-five-ish men without women.

"And how many women you got here?"

He shrugged. "Never counted."

"Thirty-two," a deep voice rumbled from across the table. "We got sixty-seven men here. Twenty-three got women, while nine of the women are sweet butts."

I twisted, seeing the beautiful man rise, his gaze locked on Audrey.

"Sweet butts?" Jo asked.

"Sluts. Club whores," Kate answered.

"They choose to be. Don't gotta but they choose it."

"And we ain't complaining!" one guy yelled, chuckles following.

Jo frowned at the beautiful man. "Audrey, what's that look like for us?"

"How many are between twenty and forty?" Audrey asked.

"Thirty-one," the guy answered immediately.

"In layman's terms it's a one in two point—actually let's just round it up to a one in three chance of partnering for these guys," Audrey said, waving a hand at the room.

"One in three is better than none," a guy muttered from behind Kate.

I looked at my sisters, a sinking feeling settling in my gut. "Are we really doing this? Giving ourselves over to men?"

Audrey tipped her head, her straight, gloriously black hair fell in long sheets over her shoulder. "I should like a man," she said, nodding to the room at large. "And these men seem as good as any. I miss sex. Though," she frowned. "If they're sharing women, I would want an STI test before sleeping with anyone. We have enough to worry about without passing syphilis or gonorrhoea around."

God grant me the wisdom to get through this.

Seriously, no filter.

I looked to Kate, finding her wide eyes fixed on a man in

a shadowed corner of the room. He was glowering at her, there was no other word for it. He looked like he was ready to throttle her, so much anger contained in his glare.

"Kate?" I asked.

She swallowed, pulling her gaze away from the man. "Thirteen p-p-percent isn't good odds. Even Ava would say th-that."

I nodded, looking at our final vote, "Jo?"

She rubbed a hand across her eyes. "I'm in. But I don't speak for my sisters. They'll have to determine what they want. We're an all or nothing package."

I looked over at Gus, meeting his blue gaze. "Your word, sir, that you'll help us and provide protection. That your men won't hurt my sisters, and that we'll be allowed to assist you by using our knowledge to better us all."

He pulled a knife free from his belt and cut the skin of his palm. He pressed it to the table, vowing, "On me life."

The next man took out his own blade, slicing his palm and pressing it to the table declaring, "On my life."

Around the table it went, each man in the room doing so.

Jo leaned over, whispering, "Is it just me or does this seem highly unhygienic considering the whole 'mutated virus' thing?"

I couldn't even find it in me to nod or laugh. Uncertainty rolled my stomach, my mouth disturbingly dry. But there was nothing I could do now. We'd sealed our fate, tying ourselves to the men in this room.

"Right." I pushed to a stand. "We've bioethanol in the trunk for you, and some fresh produce if you'll take it. But I would like to ride tonight." I glanced at my sisters, "I don't want our sisters left unprotected for longer than necessary, and we'll need to get a lot packed to transport here."

"Ye heard the lady," Gus said, raising to a stand. "Let's ride."

Chapter Three

Ellie

The ride back to the University was far different to the one leaving. For one, we were escorted by no fewer than forty men. Bikes and trucks followed our SUV through the streets, men stopping our parade to clear a path as needed.

We arrived at the College to Ava standing at the gate, gun at the ready. She looked pale and sweaty and like she should definitely still be in bed.

"The cavalry has arrived I see," she muttered, raising an eyebrow in question at the moving trucks.

"The odds are against us. Thirteen percent chance of survival. New information. We need to leave," Audrey reported, wrapping an arm around Ava, and leading her down the path to the building we'd set up as our primary residence.

"Thirteen?"

"Mm, let's talk with the others."

We'd asked the men to wait outside and they were abiding by our wishes, for now. We filled the women in, their expressions ranging from surprise to anger to upset.

"There's no other way?" Beth clarified, wringing her hands

in her apron. Jam stuck to the front in gooey globs.

"None that are viable at this point," Audrey confirmed.

"Then we're going," Ava declared, settling the issue. "We'll work things out once we get to the compound, but for now we need to take the essentials. We can come back for more but anything irreplaceable we need to take now."

"The livestock," Ruby said.

"And the food stores," Yana agreed.

"The plants and the greenhouses."

"The medication and the testing equipment." Blair added. "And I'll need everything in the lab."

"Same," I agreed.

"They have four trucks, plus what we have here. Is that enough?"

"It'll be noticeable," Ava murmured. "A full contingency of bikers plus our vehicles and the trucks? That's like throwing a thanksgiving parade and expecting no one to care."

"Do we have a choice?"

Ava rubbed a hand over her face, looking exhausted. "No. We could stagger but that would be worse. Greater potential for a tail. If we travel fast and hard, anyone watching is less likely to have time to organize and follow."

"So, we go in one hit?" Jo clarified.

"Yeah," Ava looked around the room. "How much time you need?"

"Twelve hours," Audrey said from her corner of the room. "That allows time for us to dismantle and carefully pack, as well as hide what needs to be stored until we can return."

"The animals?" Beth asked.

"We're taking them. We've got the old animal mover Jo bought with her when she arrived," Lottie said, hands cupped around a mug of steaming tea. "Can you get it working?"

The thing had been a crumbling rust bucket even before Jo had joined us, animals she'd stolen from their family's farm hollering in the back. It had sat for the last few months unused in an abandoned part of the College.

"I'll get her working," Jo promised. "But I need someone to help pack the workshop."

"Can the men assist?" Ruby asked.

"I'll check," I pushed away from the table, exiting our meeting room to find three men casually leaning against the walls of the hall. One of them was the beautiful man from Church. His patch read *Runner*, and another just above read *Treasurer*. On the other side of his worn kutte were the words *Nameless Souls MC* and a logo. Below that was their chapter—Adaminaby."U m, excuse me, Mister Runner?"

He lifted an eyebrow and the other men beside him sniggered.

"It's just Runner." His voice sent shivers straight to my core. *Stop it, Ellie!*

I swallowed, my pulse fluttering at my neck, my gaze dropping to his biceps; a tattooed snake wrapped around one arm, the other was covered in something that I couldn't quite make out from this distance.

"Are your guys okay to help us pack or do we need to factor in additional time?"

"How much you need?"

"Without you? Twelve hours."

"Fuck off," he barked. "You have one."

I sucked in a breath. "Excuse me?"

"Ain't sticking around here waiting for Purge idiots to come try their luck. You have an hour."

"If you guys help us then we need at least six," I ballparked, hoping Audrey would forgive me.

"One," he replied.

"Please, just to get the labs disassembled and properly packed is going to take at least two hours. Please, Mr. Runner—"

"Just Runner," he interrupted, his wide mouth flattening in displeasure.

"Right, Runner, sorry." I looked down, sucking in a deep breath to compose myself. "Look, if you help, we could maybe make four hours work. At a push. But we'd likely need to hide stuff and come back for it later."

I looked up, trying not to beg but knowing I was likely failing. "We just need your assistance, please."

He considered me for a long moment. His hair was in desperate need of a cut, the length curling at his ears and brushing his forehead. His beard was grown but not out of control. It gave him a wild, untamed look.

"Three," Runner finally declared. "You can have twenty guys." He looked over at one of the other men in the hall, this one had a patch that read *Soldier* and a name that said *Pope*. "Help her, set 'em to work. Prioritize the fuel. I got shit to do."

He turned on his heel and walked down the hall, leaving me with Pope and another man. The second guy was younger and had no name, just a patch that read *prospect*.

Unless Prospect is his name? But then the guy at the gate last night had the same patch. This feels like a mind teaser.

"You heard him," Pope interrupted my musing. "Where you want us to start?"

"The labs and infirmary are our priorities. But if we can get someone to help with the stores and—"

"Swift, go round up some of the boys," Pope interrupted.

Swift, not Prospect. What the hell is a prospect then? Is this like some kind of hazing ritual?

The second guy headed out.

"Follow me," I sighed, leading him back into the room. Inside, the women had used the whiteboards to prioritize our schedule.

"We've got three hours," I said glumly. "But at least we have some help."

"Three isn't enough time!" Yana cried, slapping a palm on the table.

"We'll make it work," Ava looked to Audrey. "Tell me how we can make this work."

Audrey narrowed her eyes at the board, and I marvelled once again at her brain. She rattled out a new plan and we all agreed.

"That it?" Pope asked, his blonde hair falling across his eyes.

We nodded and he tossed his head back, flashing a grin at Beth. "You need some help, gorgeous?"

"Uh-uh. No way, Bucko. You can come with me," Jo told him, grabbing his arm, and dragging him out the door. "That one is off limits to you."

He flashed Beth a wink over his shoulder, her cheeks immediately flushing. "We'll see."

"We good?" I asked the room at large.

"Yep, let's do it."

We hurried to our respective areas, men finding us. I demonstrated how to clean and pack my equipment into the containers that were stored in each room. We'd prepared for an emergency before. I winced watching them handle my delicate glasses, the beakers beautiful but breakable. Glass was incredibly hard to find in the after.

"You done?" Runner asked from the door hours later. He'd

been periodically checking in with us, making sure the packing was progressing and no one was fucking around.

I looked up from where I was placing the final few items into my container. A quick glance showed a stripped room but for some final beakers. The men who had helped me were surprisingly efficient. I'd sent them off to load my containers.

"Umm, actually yes. This is the last box." I gestured at the glassware on the final shelf. "Just these to go."

He came in, reaching for a glass and watching as I carefully rolled it in newspaper, then mimicking my movements.

He felt larger than life in this room. Taking up the space in a way I found both intimidating and intriguing.

"What's a prospect?"

He glanced, up, a small smile playing at his mouth. "Think of it like a probation period. You don't become a patched member until you prove yourself."

I tilted my head to the side, hands rolling the glass in the paper. "Patched member?"

He paused, tapping the logo on his chest, and jerked a thumb towards his back. "A full member of the club. It requires you to prove yourself. Prove your loyalty to the club. You're gonna be our brother, we gotta know you can be counted on to have our backs."

I nodded, my hands moving once more. "So, you get the logo when you're voted in?"

He shook his head. "Shit girl, don't ever call it a logo around the brothers."

I blinked. "Sorry, I didn't mean to offend. What's it called?"

"Call it a patch. Or if you need to, an emblem or symbol. Logos are what products slap on a brand so someone will buy their shit." He laid a hand over the patch on his chest. "This?

Any one of these men would lay down their lives to protect this club. It's more than something someone's slapped together in five minutes."

I nodded. There was a strange beauty in that sentiment. Both tragic and wonderous.

"That's... beautiful. Thank you for sharing."

He glanced up, his hands halting on the paper. He watched me for a moment then nodded. "You got any more questions, you come to me, Blondie. Or Kate. We'll keep you outta hot water."

I nodded again, my gaze dropping to my hands, both of us working in the easy quiet to finish.

"My name's Ellison, by the way." I told him, reaching for the final beaker. "Most people call me Ellie."

He looked at me, his face unreadable. "You done now?"

More than slightly miffed, I looked around. Everything of use had been stripped from the lab, leaving only bare walls and empty tables.

My heart gave a little tug at the sight.

"Yeah."

"Great," he waited for me to close the lid before he lifted it. "Your friends done?"

I shrugged. "Not sure."

"Better be, don't like this. This place ain't safe."

I fell in beside him, reaching absently for a stray text book by the door, wrapping my arms around it, holding it close to my chest. Probably useless in the grand scheme of things, but the familiarity of paper and the heavy weight of it in my arms felt reassuring.

"It's been safe for nine months. Ava made sure of that."

He snorted, dismissive arrogance rolling off him in waves.

"That woman's the only decent fighter among you. Anyone can see that you got lucky."

I bit my tongue, choosing not to argue. He'd find out soon enough we weren't silly, helpless women.

We made it to the trucks, joining the cacophony of sound and movement as we finalised our preparations.

Kate pulled a cart down the walk, the man who'd watched her in the meeting shadowed her steps, his arms equally full.

"Books!" she cried, looking frantic. "I got what I could. What I thought would be most useful and some fiction but—"

"Just load them," Ava said looking worse than she had earlier in the evening. "But hurry, we need to go."

As we loaded the last few items, Beth, Ruby and Lottie were moving the cattle onto the truck.

"We ready?" I asked, looking around.

All nods.

We took a second, saying silent farewells to our home.

"Time to go," Ava finally said, turning to make her way to the SUV.

I went to follow but Runner took my arm, pulling me with him.

"On my bike," he said.

I blinked. "Excuse me?"

"No room." He nodded at the trucks and vehicles. "Some of you gotta ride."

"You got a helmet?"

He sniggered. "No, but don't worry, sweetheart. I'll take good care of that cute butt."

Chapter Four

Runner

The curvy blonde clung to me as we rode through the silent streets, the only sound the rumble of the trucks and the echoing roar of the bikes.

As we hit the open road, leaving the outskirts of the abandoned coastal town, I opened her up. We'd been conserving fuel for months, but with this woman's biofuel in her tank, my baby was ready to roar.

Ellie huddled closer behind me, her breasts pushing into my back, her arms locking tighter around my stomach.

I tried to ignore the hard-on pressing against my zipper.

Concentrate on the ride, not on who you want to ride.

Easier said than done. I couldn't ignore the fact this woman was the first to be on the back of my bike since the before. The first I'd wanted on my bike since long before the dark.

But that changes today.

My ride rumbled under me, the beautiful sound another reminder of the wonders of the woman currently death-gripping my stomach.

I slowed slightly, shifting to a cruise as around me, my

brothers did the same, falling into line, shooting each other grins even while we kept watch for dangers lurking in the dark.

Eleven women, a boon. But the one behind me, the woman who could conjure fuel was a fucking miracle.

She'll be in demand.

I knew that. She had a curvy body and full lips that looked infinitely fuckable. But couple that with her knowledge? The brothers would want her. All of them. Didn't matter if she was frigid, they'd take her to get their hands on her knowledge.

The dirt turn-off to the compound came up, and a third of our party peeled off, following the road.

"Where are we going?" Blondie called from behind me, her words snatched away by the wind.

"Gotta make sure we don't got a tail," I called back. She shivered, burrowing back into me and I took a moment to appreciate her braless state.

Underwear was hard to come by in the after.

Thank fuck.

We rumbled down the backroads, curving through the thick woodland until we reached another milestone marker. The second group turned off, disappearing into the thick trees.

Blondie's arms twitched around my stomach.

Scared, Baby Girl? You should be.

Finally, I pulled off, following the last of our pack as we travelled down the dirt road, our bikes roaring through the quiet night. Not exactly subtle, but we'd be hard to follow.

We entered the east wing of the compound, the prospects holding the gate open and waving us through. I drove straight to the bunk house, ignoring the main gathering over at headquarters.

I wanted this hot piece off my bike and in my bed. Now.

I kicked out the stand, expertly parking my ride then patting Blondie's knee. "Off, Baby Girl."

She hopped off, her legs a little unsteady as she stumbled away.

I grinned, anticipation heating my blood as I reached for her, settling hands on either side of her ample hips. "Careful, Blondie. Don't want to hurt that pretty butt."

She flushed, looking off towards headquarters where the other women were gathering, directing the unloading of cattle, calling for assistance, protesting arrangements, and generally making a raucous.

I pulled her closer, grinning at her wide-eyed look of surprise as I settled her between my legs.

"W-what are you doing?" she asked, her hands fluttering uncertainly in front of her.

"Claiming what's mine." I pulled her in, fisting her hair in my hand, tilting her head to capture her lips in a brutal kiss before my brothers, the sky, and all the fucking gods.

Her body stiffened for a moment before she melted under me, her body swaying into mine and pressing tight. Her lips opened and I dove in, seizing my opportunity. She tasted like cherries and mint, and kissed me like she was born to do it.

Fuck, I need her under me.

I jerked back, ripping my mouth free and leaned down, hoisting her up and over my shoulder. In two strides I was headed to my room, ignoring the jeering men around me and the outraged cries from the women in the distance. I paid attention to the woman on my shoulder, the one panting and squirming as I carried her up the stairs, past the rooms of my brothers to my private quarters on the third floor. Spacious, clean, and fucking sound proof.

Not once did she protest.

Inside, I kicked the door shut and strode through the sitting room, kitchen, and into my bedroom, tossing her on the generous king bed. She landed with a little bump, pushing up to stare at me, her lips already red and a little swollen.

"Say no right now and you can leave. You say nothing and this is happening," I warned, panting as I started to slowly unbuckle my belt.

She flushed, chewing on one corner of her mouth as her gaze dropped to my hands.

"Say it," I repeated.

Slowly, oh so fucking slowly, she looked up. With a shaking hand she reached up to her mouth, pretending to zip it closed and throw away the key.

"Good girl."

Chapter Five

Ellie

What am I doing!?

My inner voice raged at me, demanding answers for why I was letting this big, potentially dangerous, stranger strip me of my clothing.

But a deeper, darker part of me, the part I'd found myself seeking in the days and months since the before, that part wanted this.

She *demanded* it.

Runner kissed me as if he were dying. As if I were his last meal, his last breath, his last thought. It felt intoxicating, delicious. Thrills of sparking, hot awareness raced down my body to pool low in my core.

My clit throbbed, my body pulsed, and I needed him to touch me with that possessiveness that had defined the last few moments.

Riding on his bike, cruising through the dark, the feeling of eyes upon us, the feeling of vulnerability, the loss and grief at leaving our only home, it had piled upon me until I was intensely aware of my own mortality. Of the risk and unending loss that stretched before me.

This was the after. In the after there was no reward without immense sacrifice.

I knew tonight would be a reward for me. Knew tonight would result in an as yet unknown sacrifice, yet that dark whisper didn't care.

Give in. Let him do this. You need it. No, you deserve it.

I did. I deserved to let go and find some joy, or at least pleasure, in the after. For months I'd been on the edge of fear; living in a world where my friends depended on me to contribute, to build, to create. There were no sick days, no days off. Nothing but the endless struggle to improve our situation and the constant battle with fear. God, I was so tired of being brave. Of being fearful. Anxious. Cautious. Terrified.

I needed this outlet. I needed Runner to switch off my overactive mind. To take away all thoughts and allow nothing but him to dominate my senses.

Riding into the compound, surrounded by rough men with hungry eyes and hard bodies, was the first time in over nine months that I felt comfortable to let myself go. I gave into Runner's orders. Let him take charge, allowed him to control and move me, taste, and feel me any way he desired.

And I *revelled* in it.

He stripped me, our mouths gasping, tongues tangling as I submitted to him. His hands found my breasts and we both groaned as he cupped them.

"You need this as much as I do," he growled against my lips. "You're killing me, Baby Girl."

I arched under him, my head falling back, hips tilted, desperate for him to do more.

His fingers grazed my nipples, shuddering moans escaping

from between my lips at his touch. One hand dropped to my jeans, his body shifting as he began to undo the buttons at my fly.

"Gonna fuck you good," he promised, flicking the buttons open even as he continued to tease my breast. "You fucked anyone since the before?"

I shook my head, forcing my eyes open to watch him. He studied me, his hands halting. "You fuck anyone in the before?"

I nodded, failing to tell him there had only been one, a guy I thought I'd loved. He'd turned out to be a mistake I still regretted.

"You clean? On protection?"

"I'm clean, but no. I'm not on birth control."

"Gotcha," he reached over my head, pulling out his bedside drawer and ripping free some condoms. "Tomorrow," he said casually as he laid them beside me and resumed pulling off my pants. "You go see your doctor friend. Get her to put you on birth control."

"I'm not sure we—"

He twisted me a little, enough to get access to my left butt cheek and slap it.

I froze, my butt smarting from the tap but also, strangely, I felt... relief? The feminist in me rebelled, rejecting the idea. Horrified I could feel anything but outrage at the tap. But there was a whisper of carnality that gloried in what Runner had just done. A sensual fluidity pervading my limbs, a little mew of pleasure escaping from between my lips as the heat and admonishment fed my need for release.

Runner glanced at me, his gaze dark. "You like being punished, Baby Girl?"

"I... I'm not sure."

Yes.

He rocked back on his heels, pulling my underwear and jeans free. "Guess we better find out."

Naked beneath him, he shifted, pressing two fingers to my clit, chuckling as I moaned, my legs clamping around his hand, keeping him there.

"Baby Girl, you're soaked." He pulled his hand free, bringing his fingers to his face, inhaling then sucking them clean. "I'd say you fucking love it."

He rolled me to my knees, pulling me up on all fours. I glanced over my shoulder, nervous tension radiating from me in waves.

He backed me to the edge of the bed, slipping off then pulling his own pants free and kicking them away. He turned back to me, hands running up and over the curve of my arse, the dip of my lower back, tracing my spine up to the nape of my neck. He cupped it, squeezing gently.

"You ever had a safe word before?" he asked, one hand still holding my neck, the other gliding up and down my back.

"No."

"We're gonna play tonight, you and me, and it might get rough. You feel me?"

I tried to nod but his hand halted my movement. I made a sound of affirmation instead.

"Good girl. You like what I do, you don't have to say anything but encouragement. You need a minute, you say yellow and I slow it down. But you don't like what I do, it hurts or you want it to stop, you say red. Got it?"

"Yes, Runner."

"Fuck, like the way you say that, Baby Girl."

His hand fell away from my neck, dipping to catch the strands of my hair that had escaped my ponytail, gently he pulled them back, gathering the mass at the back of my neck.

"Now, we're gonna play a little game of truth and lies. You tell me the truth, I reward you." His free hand caressed one of my butt cheeks lovingly. "But you tell me a lie, you get punished." That same hand drew back and slapped my arse, drawing a gasp from me and leaving a hot bite of pain in its wake.

I purred at the heat of his mark, craving more. More heat, more discipline… just, *more*.

"Say, yes, Runner."

"Yes, Runner," I repeated, not recognizing the raw need in my voice.

"Good girl." He rewarded me with a kiss to my arse, his lips pressed gently to the smarting skin. Silk and iron. Heat and cool. It felt inexplicably welcome. My pussy clenched in response and I could barely bite back the whimper.

"Now, first question. How long you been at that school?"

Chapter Six

Ellie

How long you been at that school?

I suddenly understood his intention. This wasn't just about sex. This was about information. My body tensed, and he chuckled, the hand in my hair pulling enough to lift my head, the pinprick of pain enough to warm my blood, further fuelling my anger.

"Don't worry, Baby Girl." He pressed his erection into my arse. "The questions are to learn more about you. Doesn't mean I'm not turned-the-fuck-on."

I hesitated, on a precipice between wanting to answer and be rewarded, and fearful of what he might ask.

Am I here for information or sex?

"Remember your safe word, Ellie." His breath felt hot as he ran his tongue up my spine, tingles following the delicious sensation.

"I was there for four years before this went down."

He released my hair a fraction, his free hand moving down to graze against my pussy lips.

"And since?"

"Since the world ended," I whispered. "I never left."

His hand cupped my pussy. I wiggled but his hand tightened on my hair keeping me in place.

"You safe at the University?"

I bit my lip, uncertain about how to answer.

Quick as a flash he removed his hand delivering a sharp slap to my arse and I jumped, squirming, wet heat beginning to coat my thighs.

"Too slow, Baby Girl. Let's try again." He rubbed the smarting spot. "Were you safe?"

"For the most part," I answered, struggling to be truthful. "Ava protected us and taught us how to protect ourselves."

"But you ran into trouble." His hand caressed my arse and I relaxed.

"Occasionally, mostly people who didn't think thirteen women could look after themselves." I twisted to look over my shoulder at him. "We took care of it."

He raised an eyebrow, his gaze dark and hungry. "How?"

I dropped my gaze, my head swinging back around, my fisted hair stopping me from dropping my head. "We... we just took care of it."

I didn't want to talk about it. The memories would kill my mood, already I could feel that blissful sense of relief disappearing.

I could feel him considering me, considering the answer I'd given him. Finally, he rewarded me by dragging a finger through my wetness, finding my clit, and rubbing.

"I'll let you get away with that tonight," Runner told me, his big finger manipulating me, rebuilding the tension between us. "Next time I ask, I expect details. Got me?"

I closed my eyes, making a noise of agreement even as all

my concentration centred on his movements. He played me expertly, my knees and arms buckling as my body responded, a gush of wetness flooding his fingers.

"That's it, Baby Girl. Go with it."

He teased and taunted; his big, blunt fingers, calloused and rough, pushed me higher, working me to the edge then halting. I whimpered, pushing back, searching for his hand. Runner chuckled, keeping just out of my reach.

"Final question." He leaned down, the heat of his body searing my back as his breath brushed the shell of my ear, his lips grazing as he whispered his question.

"Are you mine, Baby Girl?"

Goosebumps prickled across my skin, shudders wracking my body as I struggled to think past the haze of lust, struggled to control my need enough to answer.

"Yes."

He drew back immediately and for a moment I was bereft of his warmth. For a moment I felt disconnected, lost and alone. Then he was there, his hands heaving me back towards him, his cock finding my core.

"Brace, Ellie."

I had seconds to stiffen my arms before Runner thrust into me, his cock large, long, and brutal as it entered me, claiming, and marking, stretching, and fucking with raw intensity.

"Fuck," Runner swore, holding my hips steady as he fucked me hard. "Tight as a fucking glove, Baby Girl. Gonna stretch you real good."

I fell to my elbows, head burrowing into the bed as screams shredded my throat, his body dominating mine.

All I could think, all I could feel was Runner.

Runner thrusting into me. Runner pushing me to my limits.

Runner, Runner, Runner.

One hand dropped from my hips to my pussy, and he curled a hand in, pressing my clit.

"Fucking come. Now," he ordered.

At his words I shattered under him, my body breaking into a million pieces. I couldn't process anything beyond the pleasure splintering through my body and the grunting thrusts of him emptying inside me.

He collapsed on me a moment later, his big body pressing mine into the bed, his teeth sinking into my shoulder, his breath rough as he marked me. Not hard enough to bruise, but hard enough to make his intention clear.

I'm his.

The realization of my actions settled.

In the after there was no reward without immense sacrifice—and today I was the sacrifice.

Fuck.

Chapter Seven

Runner

Fuck. I mean... well, fuck.

Ellie had wrung me dry. I'd never come that hard before. Not even close.

I rolled off her, pushing to my feet. I needed to get her cleaned up. I needed to go again.

Immediately.

I headed for the bathroom, disposing of the condom. I grabbed a rag for her then froze, the hair on the back of my neck prickling.

Something's wrong.

I reached under the sink, pulling the hand gun I stashed there free. I flicked the safety off and raised it, slowly walking back to the door.

Ellie remained crumpled on the bed. Her arse pink, my handprints visible on her ample cheeks. Her hair spilled across the bed, her body in the same position I'd left her, calm and at ease.

A brush of movement to my left had me pivoting, my gun trained on the woman pointing her own weapon at me. Her

50

eyes narrowed; her hands steady as she stared me down.

"Ava," I greeted, ice running through my veins. "You wanna put that down?"

"You wanna explain why Ellie has marks on her?"

Out of the corner of my eye I saw Ellie move, heard her gasp then begin to scramble.

"Ellie, stay where you are," I ordered, not wanting her anywhere near this woman and her gun.

"Ellie, get behind me," Ava ordered, her glare promising me retribution. "Now."

Ellie pulled a blanket from the bed wrapping it around her as she fumbled to her feet, calling, "Ava, it's not what you—"

"Behind me!" Ava ordered, her gaze not wavering from me for even a moment.

"No," Ellie replied, coming to stand beside me.

"Excuse me?" Ava's gaze flicked to her then immediately to me. "Ellie, what the fuck are you doing?"

"It's not what you think," Ellie told her again, reaching a hand out to lay it on my arm. "Runner didn't hurt me."

Ava huffed out a bitter laugh. "Honey, I saw the handprints."

Ellie flushed, her body drifting closer to mine. "Umm, yeah, they were consensual."

I saw Ava's dark eyes widen, her forehead crinkling. "You sure about that?"

Ellie chuckled nervously. "Pretty sure. I mean… the orgasms were good."

I didn't relax my stance, didn't move except to ask, "Only good?"

Ellie rolled her eyes. "Fine, great."

Ava remained unconvinced, her expression unchanged.

Ellie sighed, turning slightly away from me, and making

a movement I couldn't quite catch. A second later the gun lowered and Ava flicked the safety.

I dropped my arm, doing the same.

"You wanna cover up?" Ava asked, nodding at my crotch.

I leaned against the doorjamb, giving her an eyebrow raise. "My room, my rules."

"Jesus." She turned away from me, pegging Ellie with a look. "You're sure?"

Ellie nodded. "I'm fine, Ava. Promise."

She blew out a breath, reaching a hand up and running it through her chestnut hair. "Well damn." She dropped her hand. "Guess I better go smooth some feathers."

"Ava." Ellie leaned into me, wrapping an arm around my waist. "What did you do?"

"What I had to." She pivoted on her heel, slinging the gun over her shoulder, and calling, "Later."

I watched her pull open my door and yell down the hall, "She's fine. Stand down!"

"Jesus," I muttered, looking down at Ellie. "What did she do?"

Ellie sighed, tucking a strand of her hair back. "Most likely took out a few of your guys. Ava's incredible. And scary."

"Scary?"

Ellie lifted one shoulder in a half-shrug. "She did… what do they call it in movies? Wet work?"

"What?" I barked, throwing a look at my closed door. "She's an assassin?"

"What? No! Ava does the, you know." Ellie raised a hand making a pew-pew sound as she pretended to shoot her finger gun. "She took care of stuff."

"What kind of stuff?" I asked, turning to Ellie, and backing her towards the bed.

"You know, stuff."

The back of her knees hit the bed and she went down, the blanket slipping free, her glorious tits spilling out.

"Mm," I murmured, leaning over her. "Do we need another game of truth or lies?"

She shook her head, her body flushing.

"Then you better keep that mouth busy," I told her, reaching down to fist my cock. "You ready?"

"Yes, Runner."

I fed her my cock, her lips closing around me, hot, wet perfection engulfing my length.

Fuck, I could get used to this.

Chapter Eight

Ellie

The smell of cooking woke me. I lay in the bed for a moment, my stomach rumbling as I took stock of my body. I ached, but in the most satisfying of ways. Runner had broken down my walls, easily controlling me and my pleasure.

I can't even feel ashamed.

And I didn't. I owned the way I felt around Runner. For the first time in a long time, I felt... free.

I rolled out of bed, groaning as I climbed to my feet, my body protesting in places I'd forgotten existed.

Well, you remember now, naughty girl.

Satisfaction radiated through my middle as I searched for clothes. Mine had disappeared and I hadn't had a chance to bring any up with me when we'd started last night. I found a shirt and pulled that on, grimacing when my breasts pressed against Runner's shirt. He may be tall and muscular but the man was lean, and my breasts? Not at all small.

"It'll do," I muttered, wandering towards the kitchen and the delicious smells wafting my way.

Runner's apartment was surprisingly large. A decent sitting

room, a separate bedroom with full sized wardrobe and sitting area, a large bathroom (though no tub), and a kitchen. I had a feeling this apartment hadn't always been like this. The floors were newish and the kitchen looked like it had been upgraded in the last few years.

"Hey," Runner called from the stove. "You like bacon?"

I froze, blinking at him. "Bacon?"

"Yeah, you want some?"

"Fuck yes," I replied, hurrying to the bar stools, and sliding onto one. "How the hell do you have bacon?"

"Wild pigs." He plated a bunch of food, handing it over. "Pigs, not hogs. They're everywhere around here. We figure there must have been a piggery that they escaped from at some point. Breeding like fiends too."

"Did you check them for worms?" I asked, wrinkling my nose at the plate.

"Babe, we got hunters galore. They know what's good meat and what ain't."

I examined my meat for a moment but the delicious smell and mouth-watering memory of bacon finally won me over and I forked a piece, groaning as it hit my tongue.

"This," I said to Runner, my eyes closed, "is ecstasy."

He made his way over to where I sat, taking the seat beside my own, pulling his chair close as he teased me. "Baby, you said that last night while I was balls deep. Make up your mind."

I sniggered, bumping him with my shoulder then forking another piece. He'd paired it with eggs and toast, strong coffee, and some watered-down juice concentrate.

"That was a regular feast," I said pushing my plate away at the end of the meal and resting one hand on my very full belly. "Thank you."

He lifted our plates, carrying them to the sink and dropping them in. "Gotta feed you after last night." He tossed me a grin. "You earned it after that last round."

I blushed at the memory, knowing even the roots of my hair had to be red.

In the last round he'd made me come so hard I'd squirted—a feat never before achieved. I'd passed out soon after, my body completely wrecked by his hunger.

"You want a shower?"

I grimaced, pulling at his shirt. "Yeah, I smell like sex."

He came back around, turning me in my seat until he could step between my thighs, his hands settling on my waist.

"I happen to like the way you smell," he whispered, his gaze shockingly hungry. "And the sight of you in my shirt."

I had no reply. My poor abused pussy clenched, my body wanting him again.

Down, girl.

"But your girls are gonna need proof of life, and God knows what shit that woman pulled last night." He pressed closer to me, one hand sliding down to hover above my abdomen. I wanted to arch into him, let him touch me again. Instead, I remained absolutely still, knowing if I moved, he'd not hesitate to punish me.

A satisfied smirk tugged at his lips. "Good girl, you're learning."

I hated that his praise warmed me and made me wet. The feminist in me raged against it.

But the carnal, sensual, primitive me preened. I craved his approval and was willing to do more, a fuck load more, to achieve it.

He dropped his hand, one finger grazing through my obvious

arousal. We both groaned and he chuckled.

"Naughty, naughty girl." He pulled his hand away, raising his finger to his lips and licking it clean. "Go clean up, I'll get your shit."

It was only then that I realised he had already showered. His clothes were new, and his body smelled of deodorant and soap.

"Right," I muttered, hopping down from the stool, and making a beeline for the shower. It was the first time since entering that I wondered about my own appearance.

Nine months without a hairdresser or waxing salon was one thing. But I'd spent nearly twenty-four hours the previous day travelling then packing then on the back of a motorcycle. I couldn't have been daisy fresh when he took me.

"Ellie," Runner called from the doorway just as I stepped into the bathroom. I stuck my head back out, raising an eyebrow in question.

"Don't you think for one goddamned second I don't want to fuck you raw and keep you locked in this bedroom for the next three weeks. As much as I wanna do that, you're an asset. You got skills that the club needs. They've given me this morning. They're not gonna let me take the rest of the day without payment. You feel me?"

I started to nod then shook my head.

"All you need to know, Baby Girl, is that we all pull our weight around here but some are more valuable than others. It's my job as Treasurer to weigh it all up and work out an equitable outcome. And you, darlin'?" His eyes flashed. "You're worth more than all of us combined."

With that he walked out of the room, the door clicking shut and automatically locking behind him.

I stared at the door for long moments, replaying his words.

Warmth stole over me, burrowing deep into the places I'd locked away since the before. The golden glow of his praise rushing over them, filling all the holes, and repairing parts of me I hadn't even realised were broken.

You're worth more than all of us combined.

Well, damn.

Chapter Nine

Ellie

Runner had returned with a bunch of guys, and yelled at me to stay in the bathroom while they settled my things in his rooms.

I didn't want to question it, but I assumed this meant that I was staying with him. I wasn't quite sure how I felt about that just yet.

On one hand, orgasms. On the other, the guy was practically a stranger.

A deliciously attractive stranger who smelled nice, cooked me breakfast and had a cock the size of—

"Ellie," Runner interrupted my thoughts. "You paying attention?"

We were standing in an empty warehouse at the back of the compound's property. There were five side by side, each in decent but not perfect repair.

"Yes," I lied, then immediately flushed when I caught his raised eyebrow.

He leaned in, whispering in my ear, "That's one."

I shivered my body clenching in response to his warning. I caught Ava watching me, meeting her questioning gaze briefly before immediately looking away, pretending to examine the shelving units in the giant warehouse.

Turns out the old compound had once housed over five thousand soldiers, and was about fifty times bigger than I'd anticipated. After the Vietnam War, it had become excess property, eventually being offered for sale in the mid-nineties. The club had purchased it for dirt cheap after a developer had been informed that the surrounding national park rendered the property undevelopable.

They'd done a good job of keeping the buildings, various sheds, and whatnot in good repair. But it was a lot of property to maintain and they'd lost members to the virus.

Runner and a group of men he'd failed to introduce were showing us around the property, giving us the grand tour and discussing where we should set up our various workshops.

Jo had stayed behind, having already found the mechanic's workshop. We'd left her in a deep discussion with a guy called Bull about something to do with engine performance.

The club had done a good job shoring up fencing and initiating patrols in the after. They had a giant property, but the back half was taken up by the edge of a lake, cutting the area they needed to patrol.

I knew Ava was already speaking to them about rotating us on to guard duty. I didn't look forward to it, it had definitely been one of my least favourite tasks.

"None of these will work for me," Blair said, running a hand over a dusty workbench. "They're not sterile enough. If you want me to operate an actual medical lab, then I need airtight housing."

"We got Butcher," one of the guys muttered, kicking a shelving unit. "You could settle in with him."

Blair frowned, "You have a butcher?"

"Not *a* butcher, we *got* Butcher. He's our current doc. Got a set-up back at the compound. You'd have to check but he might have room for you."

Blair blew out a frustrated breath. "And you didn't tell me this before because…?"

The kid shrugged, not offering her an answer.

Blair shot me a look that asked for me to step in, and I once again questioned the sanity of last night's actions.

The longer today went on, the more it seemed that I'd become an unofficial bridge between the club and the women—a position I had no wish to adopt.

"You said you had a farm here?" Beth asked. "Can we see that?"

Her animals had been penned up near the outbuildings last night, but we'd need a more permanent home for them shortly.

"Babe, follow me and you can see anything you like."

Immediately eight pairs of eyes shot laser beams at Pope, all of us well aware of Beth's inexperience with the opposite sex. To say we were protective was an understatement.

"I'll come with you," Audrey announced, her gaze locked on Pope. "You'll need me."

"For?" Pope asked, crossing his arms over his chest.

"Don't know yet. But I know you'll need me. Everyone does, eventually," Audrey replied, pushing her glasses up her nose. "Lead on, if you please."

Pope considered her for a moment and I had to hide a smile. He looked at her as if she were a fascinating bug that might bite.

"Follow me," he finally said, turning and leading Beth and Audrey outside.

"Will this work?" Runner asked me, nodding at the cavernous space.

"For the biofuel, yeah. We'll need to tidy it up, but with this much space I might be able to increase production—if we can get the right resources."

"Whatcha need?"

"Well, it depends on what you can get me. Corn would be great. Orange peels or tobacco, at a pinch but it would take longer for me to reproduce the correct enzyme and then engineer. If you can get your hands on soybeans or vegetable oil then I might be able to generate some biodiesel, but that depends on other factors like—"

"Just write down what you need, the quantities you need it and we'll get it for you."

I blinked. "You'll get it for me?"

"Yeah"—Runner glanced at his watch—"that's what we do."

"Runner," I chuckled nervously. "I think you underestimate what we need. I had to order corn for months. A bushel of corn only produces about ten and a half litres, which means—"

"Babe, make the list, we'll get what you need."

I chewed my lip. "Just… just don't blame me if this doesn't work, okay?"

He wrapped an arm around my neck, pulling me into him. "You worried it won't work?"

"I'm worried about getting the bits to make it work. If I have everything then we'll be fine."

"Then you'll have everything," he said, as if it were simple.

"But—"

"Stop," he ordered. "Baby Girl, I'm telling you, we got this. Trust me."

I relaxed into him, letting him take over once again. Enjoying the freedom that came from him being in charge.

I could get used to this.

It was an intoxicating thought, allowing Runner to own me. To be the person who had complete control.

It wasn't that I wanted to be a damsel in distress, nah, I was too practical for that. It was the temptation to allow someone else to be the worrier and the warrior in the relationship that called to me. There was a freedom, a release that came with him being in charge.

And God help me, it was fast becoming an addiction.

He squeezed my arse then stepped back, capturing my hand, and pulling me after him.

"Got a surprise for you," he told me. We walked through the long warehouse to the rear, leaving our party behind. Runner opened a door, helping me step out and avoid the rusted edges.

"What am I—Oh." I gasped, staring in shock.

"Yeah." He grinned. "Told you."

There were three large grain silos nestled in behind the warehouses. They'd been blocked from view by the buildings. Beside them sat a small shed, some good quality farm equipment, including a harvester and two tractors, parked inside. But it was what lay behind the buildings that really got my attention.

"Corn," I whispered, reaching up a hand to shield my eyes. "You guys grow corn."

Rows and rows of the baby plants lined a paddock, stretching out for at least a mile. The angle of the building had hidden the cleared field from view, the bush providing additional cover around us.

"Runner." I looked up at him, feeling the first bloom of hope uncurl. "This is gonna work."

"You sure?" he asked with a smile. "A second ago, you said—"

I slapped him on his stomach, a laugh erupting quickly from him. He grabbed me around the waist, lifting me and spinning me around. After a moment, he let me slide down his body, pressing me into him. He dropped his forehead to mine, our breath mingling.

"You're gonna change our fortunes, Baby Girl. I can feel it."

I gulped. "I hope so."

"Baby, you know it. Own that shit." He gently tapped the side of my head. "You got a brain in there, it's gonna serve you well."

I nodded, our heads bopping together with my movement.

"Now, gotta get you back, gotta get that list, then we're gonna eat, and then fuck. Complaints?"

I shook my head, desire pooling low at his words.

"Good girl." With that muttered praise, he kissed me, his body warm, hard, and big, his lips demanding and hungry.

And I rejoiced in him.

Chapter Ten

Runner

We never made it to the bedroom. First distraction was lunch. The mess hall was normally a mismatch of people trailing through at odd hours. Not today. Today the joint was packed with people, all of them exclaiming over the new chef's offerings.

"What the fuck?" I asked, inhaling the delicious aroma of a decent meal. "Who's cooking today?"

"That'd be Yana," Ellie laughed beside me. "The woman can turn scraps into a gourmet meal."

"You had a chef? They did that at your fancy college?"

"She's Aella's sister."

"Who?"

"Our nurse. She was studying, Yana came to live with us."

I scratched my chest. "You not only got a group of women together, but you actively recruited from outside the uni?"

"Well, yeah." Ellie picked up two trays, handing one to me then followed the line of hungry bikers down to the serving station.

"Our success scenarios relied on us getting the right mix of people. And fact is, no one expects much of women. I mean, look at Jo, Ruby and Beth. They're three of the most incredible women, but their brothers are the ones who get to work the farm, their family didn't even want them to go to university or get a trade. They were all told to find a man and pop out kids. But they're so much more than their uterus."

"So, they're all related?"

"Mm, sisters."

"Why didn't they go be with their people?"

Ellie sighed, reaching for a pair of tongs to place fresh bread rolls on our plates.

"When the world started going dark, Beth and Ruby were told not to bother coming home. The family lives together on a big old ranch. There are thirteen kids, ten boys, three girls. Jo was the only girl who still lived in town, though she had her own apartment at her mechanic's workshop. The boys all lived with their wives and families in separate houses on the farm. Religious folk, but also gun toting. They didn't have time for three unwed girls. Told Jo that unless she wanted to shack up with one of the farm hands then she wasn't welcome either."

I thought of the spitfire woman with the gruff demeanour and shook my head. Couldn't imagine she'd taken to that direction well.

We passed through the line, heaping food on our plates then found a table in the main area. A few men surrounding us, sending curious glances Ellie's way.

They knew by now I'd claimed her, didn't stop them from being curious about her though and I couldn't fault them for that. She was beautiful, sure. But she was also new, an extreme rarity since the before. Unless a brother nomad was passing through, strangers were few and far between.

Pope slapped down a tray, dropping beside me with a heavy sigh. Audrey and Beth followed, immediately settling on his other side.

He tossed a look my way. "This one," he grumbled as he hooked a finger at Audrey. "Is fucking crazy."

She rolled her eyes, picking up her fork. "You only say that because you don't understand higher thinking."

"Baby, I don't need to understand your intellectual jargon to figure out that you're fucking crazy."

Ellie opened her mouth ready to ask but I held up a hand, stopping her.

"Ignore him," I directed, well versed in Pope and his idiosyncrasies. "He's an idiot."

"Hey!" Pope protested but I ignored him, turning instead to Ellie with a question.

"So, you got the three sisters, and the chef and the nurse, anyone else related?"

Ellie nodded, swallowing a bite of her meal. "Blair, our doctor, is my sister. And there's Ava and Lottie. That's it."

I savoured the delicious chili; their chef had managed to produce the best goddamned meal I'd tasted in over nine months.

"What about your family?" Pope asked, shamelessly eavesdropping. I sent him a warning glare but he ignored me.

"When Perth went dark, and then Brisbane, we realised this was getting serious, we reached out to our families. But most of us are from out of state, and things were changing so rapidly. States going into total lock down, friends and family being diagnosed, then cities going dark, we realised pretty quick we were safer where we were. Most of us managed to say goodbye before the blackouts." Ellie swallowed, looking away. "We told them where we were and our plans to stay put. They've had nine months to find us. But no one came."

I digested that information.

"Babe, have you heard any information about Western Australia?" I asked carefully. The bikers around me, sitting up, suddenly alert.

"No, we were hoping to reconnect. Audrey's been working on a communications solution but it's been tough because she doesn't have all the parts she needs and—"

Audrey made a dismissive gesture. "These guys have the parts. Give me tomorrow and I'll have us up and running."

I absorbed that little nugget then pushed it aside, focusing on Ellie.

"We have brothers who travel all over the country. They're called nomads. When this shit went down, when cities started going dark, we activated the nomads to become messengers for our network." I turned to her fully, reaching out both my hands to capture hers. "They've been by a few times. We get one about once a month, though that's slowed in the last two."

"No fuel," Pope muttered.

"These nomads, they bring news passed through the various networks." I squeezed her hands. "Baby, Perth fell. Most of Western Australia is gone. Government did an eradication exercise to try and slow the spread. Ended in a civil war. Three months ago, a nomad passing through reported that anyone still left was making their way east but there are militia, cults, groups like The Purge, and a shit ton of preppers ready to cannibalise or kill to protect their own arses. Not to mention the desert in between." I squeezed her hands again, searching her face. "I'm sorry."

The table was silent, but I ignored them and focused on Ellie.

She swallowed, her face pale, eyes glassy as she looked at me. "What about the other cities? That's Perth. But what about the other states?"

"Similar stories," Pope replied. "Army goes in, refugees come out."

Ellie looked at me. "These nomads, are their stories consistent?"

"Yeah," I answered truthfully, hating it would hurt her. "And if their stories hadn't matched up, the shellshocked trauma that they'd been unable to shake from their faces would have clued us in."

Ellie nodded, sucking in a deep breath.

"Scenario one-eight-four," Audrey said from across the table, her fork scrapping at the bottom of her tray.

"Excuse me?" Pope asked, raising an eyebrow in her direction.

"What Runner is describing is scenario one-eight-four. My software was correct." She licked her fork then glanced around the table, blinking when she realised everyone's attention was on her.

"What?" she asked defensively. "I designed the program to give us scenarios. You don't think I'd have got it to look at potential genocide? History always repeats."

"Jesus, Audrey." Beth pushed to her feet, shoving back from the table. "I gotta go."

Audrey watched her leave, a frown on her face. She turned back to the table, asking, "Did I say something wrong?"

Ellie sighed, slipping her hands free and returning to her meal. "Honey, remember how we talked about emotional intelligence and empathy? Beth's hurting. This was unexpected news."

"Not to me," Audrey returned. "If she'd just read the full report of all possible scenarios then she'd—"

"Audrey," Ellie sighed, shaking her head. "Just because you predicted something doesn't make it easier to deal with. We all have friends and family out there. No matter that we've all assumed they're dead, it doesn't make it easier to hear."

Audrey considered Ellie's words, then shook her head, picking up a kid's juice box. She stabbed a straw in the top and sucked with gusto. When finished, she pulled back, smacking her lips together with a sigh. "People are irrational creatures."

Ellie sighed, leaning into me. "I know."

"Ah, here's me new additions," Gus boomed through the room, his arms wide in welcome as he made his way to us. "Mama wants to meet ye."

I tensed, shooting a glance at Pope. He met my gaze, one eyebrow raised in question, a frown marring his brow.

"Mama?" Ellie asked quietly.

"Prez's woman."

"Oh, I didn't realise Kate's mother lived here."

"She doesn't. She's dead." I answered, not liking that Kate hadn't filled them in on her background.

Gus made it to our side, bending down to haul Ellie to her feet and wrap her in a boisterous embrace. She glanced over his shoulder at me with wide, startled eyes. The hairs on the back of my neck lifted, but I forced myself to relax, waiting for the inevitable direction to come.

"Come, me lovebird. Mama's waiting." Gus turned Ellie and him towards the back exit of the mess hall, calling over his shoulder, "Runner, be a good boyo and sort out the Army girl. She's doing me fucking head in."

"On it," I replied, gritting my teeth as I watched him walk

away with my woman. Pope rose beside me, coming to stand close.

His voice was low as he promised, "Just a little longer, brother."

I knew it. Didn't change the fact that I wished that coming moment was now.

Fuck.

Chapter Eleven

Ellie

Gus escorted me to his apartments. Or, should I say, palatial residence. He'd turned one of the spare outbuildings into his private suite. He pointed out the fixtures, bragged about the comforts, then led me upstairs to what I assumed was a beauty salon. A gaggle of women sat inside, three of them in chairs in various states of transformation, while three others chatted with them, snipping or colouring hair.

There were two other women in the room. The first, a young woman in perhaps her early twenties, sitting behind a desk, writing. The second woman relaxed on a fainting lounge, a cocktail in one hand, a cigarette in the other. She had to be Gus' age, perhaps in her late fifties or older, but she looked amazing—her face wrinkleless, body tight. It was only the skin on the back of her hands that gave her away.

All chatter ceased as Gus and I stepped through the doors.

"Got a live one for ye, Mama." Gus said, stepping across the room to plant a kiss on the woman's lips.

"Thank you, sugar." She reached up, caressing his face. "Wendy, you wanna escort Gus out."

One of the women, perhaps in her early thirties, immediately stopped snipping, and went with Gus. I saw him slip a hand onto the small of her back as he led her out. A shiver of apprehension slid down my spine.

Mama lay back in her chair, considering me. "Come closer, honey. My eyes aren't what they used to be."

The women watched me as I stepped further into the room. The only one not looking at me was the young woman at the desk. The hair on the back of my neck prickled, setting me on edge.

"Ain't you a pretty little thing," Mama cooed. She patted the end of the lounge, gesturing for me to come sit.

I went, noting the exits and taking a mental recap of the building's layout.

"You're the fuel girl?" Mama asked, reaching for a new cigarette.

I nodded.

She lit up, taking a long drag, considering me through the smoke. "You got a name, hun?"

"Ellison," I replied, trying to act casual. "But people call me Ellie."

"Ellie, pretty name for a pretty girl." She took another drag, blowing the smoke out as she watched me. "Word is Runner's claimed you, that right?"

I flushed but nodded.

"Hm." She tapped the cigarette on a tray, a hunk of ash falling from the end. "That boy's trouble if you ask me."

"Big trouble," one of the women agreed.

"You'd be better off choosing a nicer boy. One that falls in line." She glanced at the girl behind her. "Get the list."

The girl immediately stood, walking to a shelf, and pulling

73

a book free. She opened it flicking to a page, then brought it over to Mama, laying it in her lap.

"Let's see," Mama muttered, her finger rolling down the list. I couldn't help but notice her fake nails—blood red and newly applied.

I looked down at my own hands, noting the dirt under my chipped nails, the callouses on my hands.

The after didn't give a fuck about being pretty.

"You got Ice," she said tapping a finger against a name on the page.

"Ice is Kate's," the girl protested from desk, still scribbling in her notebook.

"Shut up, girl. Ain't no one want to hear from you," Mama barked. She sniffed, shooting me a look. "Besides, Kate ain't claimed him. What ain't claimed is free game far's I'm concerned."

I blinked suddenly realizing we were discussing men and who to pair me with.

"Oh, oh!" I breathed, looking around the room. "Um, thank you. I mean, that's awfully nice of you to suggest a new partner but honestly, I'm good. Runner and I have an understanding and—"

Mama raised her hand, halting my protest. Her eyes narrowed on me. "Honey, we're your sisters now." She gestured at the room at large. "It's our responsibility to see you properly settled. Let us guide you. You ain't been here long, but it'd be real easy to have someone like Runner take advantage of you."

"He isn't, I promise. We have an understanding," I repeated. My pulse hammered in my ears, my palms sweaty, my body ready to flee at the least provocation.

I gotta get outta here.

74

Mama considered me for a long moment. The women around us remained silent, their movements stiff as they worked.

Eventually she shrugged. "Your choice, hun."

She gestured at a woman who dropped her tools, returning a moment later with a glass. She handed it to Mama who stood, moving around the back of the lounge to a pitcher on the table near the young woman. Mama refilled her own glass then mine before returning to the lounge. She held the now full glass out to me. "Here's a toast, to new beginnings."

I took it, hands trembling slightly. She clicked our glasses together then lifted hers to her mouth, taking a sip, watching me the entire time.

The young woman sitting behind Mama caught my eye, making the subtlest shake of her head.

Fuck.

"To new beginnings," I echoed, lifting the glass to my lips. I pretended to drink, conscious of the numerous eyes on me.

Get out of this, Ellie!

I coughed, my body pitching forward, spilling most of my drink on the floor. I pretended to sputter and choke on the eye wateringly strong alcohol, not a single drop having touched my tongue.

"God," I barked, "what was that?"

"The best we can do with homebrew," Mama cackled, slapping me on the back. "Shoulda told us you couldn't handle your liquor, sweetie."

The young woman with the sad eyes watched me wearily.

I waited a few more moments before finally standing. "Look, it's been lovely to meet you, but I gotta get back to my friends. If I'm to get this fuel up and running, I need to get started today."

Mama her head tilted to one side. "Mm, you do that." She twisted, barking over her shoulder, "Girl! Escort dear Ellie here home." She turned back to me, offering me a smile. "Make sure she gets there safe, got me?"

The girl nodded, pushing up from her seat. "Follow me please," she whispered, her head bowed, hair falling over her face. Her notebook clutched to her chest.

I rose, offering Mama a smile. "Thank you for the drink, and for the offer of... well, for the offer."

"You come back soon, darlin'." Mama offered graciously. "We'll fix you up real nice. And your friends too, of course."

I nodded, offering her a toothy grin—the best I could do when all I wanted was to get the fuck out. "Thank you."

"Bye, sugar, see you soon."

I followed the girl out, waiting until we were out of earshot to ask the question burning on my lips.

"Are we—" I started but she shook her head once, violently, effectively cutting me off.

I shut up, following her through the hall and down the stairs. Just as I'd suspected, Wendy was riding Gus in the living room.

"Leaving?" Gus asked, his hands on Wendy's waist as she continued to ride his cock, complete with over-the-top porn star noises.

I kept my eyes lowered, unsure of how to answer.

"She's not feeling well," the girl replied for me. "I'm taking her home."

Gus smiled. "Good girl. Take her straight there, no dallying."

The girl nodded, and led me away. I tried to ignore the fact Wendy hadn't stopped the whole time we'd been in the room. If she'd noticed us, she hadn't reacted.

76

Outside the girl led me across the yard waiting until we were in the middle of the clearing to finally speak.

"Don't react, someone might be watching," she ordered in a whisper, her head down, her hair covering her face. "Just tap your hand against your thigh if you understand me."

I did as she directed.

"Please listen closely. They put a drug in your drink. Gus'll be coming to find you soon. He 'll take you, then you'll disappear. They'll say you ran off or got lost or decided to go home or whatever they consider a plausible excuse. If you don't want that to happen, then we need to get you to Runner. Now. Where is he?"

I dipped my head, whispering, "I didn't drink it."

"But they think you did. They already had this planned. The drug kicks in, in about twenty minutes. You need to either be locked in a safe room with Runner or Gus is gonna take you, one way or another. Now, where is he?"

"He was sent to deal with my friend."

"And where is she?" the girl asked, obviously exasperated with me.

"I don't know."

The girl hesitated, her steps slowing. "Fuck it, just... stay close."

She veered off course, leading me behind three buildings, pushing us into the long afternoon shadows. She gestured at me to be quiet and stay put, peering around one building then darting across to the other, gesturing for me to follow a moment later.

I did, my heart in my throat.

She led me to a second barracks, pulling me inside, down a hall and to a door at the rear. She knocked twice, kicking it once with her shoe.

It opened, a man leaning half-naked in the doorway, pants slung low on his hips, fly undone.

"Little Mouse," he greeted taking us in. "And a stranger. Who have you brought me today?"

"This is Runner's girl. Moved her in last night. She's just been at Mama's."

The man went alert, looking at me then down the hall, snapping, "Inside."

The girl pushed me, whispering, "Go. And if they ask, you don't remember anything."

"Find Runner," the guy ordered her. "If anyone asks, I found you and brought her here." He shoved me further into the room. "Go, Mouse, now."

She nodded, taking off as he kicked the door shut, locking it, and reaching for a pistol that sat on a shelf beside the door.

Fuck.

"What's your name?" he asked, checking the barrel.

"Ellie," I said, surprised that my voice sounded normal.

"Right, Ellie, here's the deal. If Runner doesn't get here in the next few minutes shit is gonna go down. Bad shit. If anyone saw you come here then you're in danger and I'm gonna have to do some shit that will get real ugly real fast. You feel me?"

I nodded.

"Good," he gestured to his apartment. "Go in the bathroom. Lock the door. There's a gun under the sink, you know how to use a gun?"

I nodded again.

"Good. Don't come out until either Runner, Pope or me says. You hear from anyone else, you shoot the bastard. Got me?"

I nodded a third time, my hands trembling.

He tucked the pistol into the back of his jeans, placing his hands on my shoulders and giving me a little shake. "Babe, you pull it together. You can break down later, okay?"

I swallowed, sucked in a deep breath, squaring my shoulders. "Okay." I answered. "What's your name?"

"Texas," he replied letting me go and pulling the pistol back out. "In the bathroom, go."

I went, locking the door, finding the gun, and climbing into his dirty bathtub. I trained the pistol at the door, my ears pricked as I listened for movement.

Seconds turned into minutes as I waited, alert. All my focus on the door. But while my body was primed and ready, my mind raced. Scenarios on an endless loop but I kept circling back to one question.

What have I gotten myself into?

Chapter Twelve

Runner

Ava stood at the shooting range, hands on hips, glaring at me.

I glared right back; arms crossed over my chest.

"I got money on the girl," Beast muttered behind me.

"I don't know, Runner does that thing with his—"

"Runner!"

I spun, hand immediately going to the weapon at my hip.

"Mouse," Pope muttered. The hair on the back of my neck lifted, ice racing through my veins. I moved, meeting her halfway.

"Where is she?" I asked, looking over Mouse's shoulder.

"I took her to Texas."

I bolted, heading for Texas's apartment, knowing my brothers would be at my back.

If she's been harmed, Prez is dead.

"Go home, Mouse. Now!" I heard Beast order her away but I ignored them, all my attention focused on getting to Ellie.

At the barracks, I flattened against the side of the building, glancing around. Pope and Beast followed, giving me a nod.

I pulled my gun free, holding it by my side, forcing looseness into my limbs. I took one deep breath then walked around the front of the building. The place was clear, just a woman off to one side following her kid as he ran across the yard, laughing.

"Chief's woman," Pope muttered from behind me. "If she sees us, Kimi won't talk."

Not a threat.

I entered the barracks, pausing to listen.

"Go, brother," Beast ordered, taking guard at the door.

I headed for Texas's apartment, fisting it twice, calling, "It's me."

"Thank fuck," Texas growled, pulling the door open, a pistol in his hand. He jerked his head inviting me in. "She's in the bathroom."

I headed straight there, shoving my gun back in its holster, calling, "Baby Girl?"

I heard movement on the other side of the door, a lock shifting and a second later the door opened a fraction of an inch, a sliver of pale face peering out at me.

"You wanna come out, sweetheart?"

The barrel of a gun poked out, pointing straight at my chest. I heard Texas draw in a quick breath, but I ignored him, proud of my girl for protecting herself.

"Tell me, right now, Runner, what the fuck is going on."

"Baby, come on out here and—"

"No!" The gun wavered for a second then steadied. "Right now."

I heard someone enter the room behind us, but I couldn't pay attention to them, all my focus on Ellie.

"I'm sorry, baby. I didn't think they'd try it with you. Not after we all swore at Church."

"What does that even mean?" she asked, the gun still pointing

81

at me.

"Church, the meeting you went to. We promised you'd be safe. Fuck, Prez promised in front of the devil and his brothers." I ran a hand through my hair. "This is complicated."

"Then uncomplicate it, 'cause I am *not* leaving this *goddamned* bathroom until you tell me *exactly* what I've walked me and my friends into."

A gun cocked behind me and I twisted, Ava leaned against a wall, her weapon trained on me, another on Texas. She offered a narrow-eyed glare.

"Talk."

"Prez is dirty. We can't prove it, but we've got our suspicions. Problem is, boys are loyal as fuck. Mama keeps the sweet butts, orders them around like she's a fucking madam. Boys don't mind so long as they get their dick wet. She says it's to keep the girls safe but it's bullshit. It's to control who gets into the inner sanctum. It's fucking exploitative and dirty as shit."

"You said we were safe. You fucking promised me." Ellie's voice wavered.

"You are. Safer than in that fucking university with The Purge running down on you."

"And safer here than being a sitting duck for the Prez," Texas added, immediately holding up his hands in surrender when Ava jerked the gun his way. "Peace, woman. I ain't the one you need to be worried about."

"We shouldn't be fucking worried about any of you," Ava retorted. "Ellie, what you wanna do."

Her one eye watched me from the crack in the door. "Runner, speak."

"We needed bait," I admitted. "When Kate came home, we thought they'd target her. Ice has been on her since she got here."

"Ice?" Ava asked.

"One of the good guys, though the Prez don't know it. Kid's been in love with her since he was thirteen," Texas replied, arms still raised. "Sorry fucking sap."

"Explain the bait," Ellie said, drawing attention back to her.

"We needed proof. Women who turned up here were going missing. Only one or two. A few ended up as property, and we protected them, hiding them away from Mama and the Prez."

"But we didn't have proof," Texas added. "And to get excommunicated from this club? We need solid proof of wrongdoing."

"So, you hung a bunch of women out to dry?" Ava asked.

"I'm sorry," I replied, staring at Ellie. "Sorrier than you'd ever fucking know. We thought it would be Kate. I never thought they'd try it on you. Never. I claimed you."

"You don't touch another man's property," Texas added. "It's law."

Ellie's gun steadied. "But you'd let them take any of the other girls. Left them at risk?"

"Never," I growled, angry she'd even think that. "Every single one of your friends has had a man on her since she arrived.

Surprisingly, it was Ava who lowered her weapons, switching the safety on. "Well that's true. Couldn't drop that tail no matter how hard I tried."

"Ghost. He's ex-special ops. Fucking ninja if you ask—"

"Texas, you mind?"

Ellie's weapon wavered for a moment then dropped. The door opened slowly and she stared at me, her big eyes filled with hurt.

My stomach clenched. I reached for her but she darted away,

my hand grasping air.

"Ellie…."

"Ava, can I stay with you?" Ellie asked, ignoring me.

"Of course, honey." Ava glanced my way, offering me a sympathetic smile. "You wanna go now?"

"Yeah." She brushed past me, and I let her. Though it fucking killed me not to touch her.

This is too fucking important. This is about more than me and her. This is about lives.

"We need to brief the others," Ava muttered.

I shook my head. "Can't let you do that."

Ava raised an eyebrow. "Excuse me?"

"He's right," Texas said, running a hand through his hair. "We actually need you ladies here."

"As bait?" Ava stated, her expression making it pretty fucking clear that wasn't gonna happen.

"Yeah," Texas replied, leaning against a wall. "You women represent hope. Hope for fuel, hope for good fucking food, hope for maybe one of you becoming our property someday."

" Fuel, food, and fucking. It's what every girl aspires to have in a relationship. " Ava drawled, looping an arm around Ellie. " No way in hell am I risking any one of my girls."

"We've *got* you," Texas insisted.

"No, you don't," Ellie replied, squaring her shoulders, and glaring at him. She transferred that glare to me. "I walked into that… that… that *viper's nest* alone. She sized me up and expected me to just fall in line like I had no other choice. She was selecting a *man* for me. She had a book with names. She tried to *drug* me." Ellie shook her head. "Nope, I'm done. We're done. We're leaving."

The women turned, both moving to the door.

"You leave, you sentence other women to the fate you just avoided."

They froze, shoulders tightening.

"I'm serious," I stated, watching them closely. "You think we haven't tried to stop him? A brother died when we tried to mount a fucking coup. We didn't have the evidence to sway those loyal to the Prez. But nine months on and they can't ignore shit now. It's gonna take one little spark to blow this shit right up."

After a long moment Ava finally turned, but Ellie remained facing the door, her head twisted away from me.

"What are you proposing exactly?" Ava asked, crossing her arms over her chest, her face impassive.

"They tried to drug the woman that can give my brothers the one thing they desire more than anything—the freedom to ride."

"Holy fuck," Ava breathed, her eyes bugging out. "Holy fucking shit."

"She's quick," Texas muttered.

Ellie still hadn't moved.

Ava began to pace. "And if I let this happen?"

"One, it's not up to you, it's up to Ellie. Two, if Ellie agrees to it, then we'd make sure she's safe. Three, we'd give you whatever the fuck you wanted."

Ava paused, eyebrow raising. "Anything?"

"Yes," I wanted the Prez gone that fucking badly that I was willing to sell my soul to the devil.

"Ellie?" Ava asked.

"You want to drug me and then show me off." Ellie asked, though it wasn't a question.

"Yeah."

85

The room watched as she slowly turned towards me, her face pale but wiped clean of emotion.

"If I do this, I get to choose our reward?"

"I swear, baby, anything."

She stared at me for a long moment, the temperature in the room dropping, her gaze was so cold.

"I'll do it."

Chapter Thirteen

Ellie

I watched Texas pull a small lockbox from behind a false back in his bookshelf. He dialled the combination and it opened, pulling free a small baggy with two pills inside.

Ava stood beside me, her face blank as we watched him shake the bag, dropping one of the pills into a glass of alcohol.

"You still sure you want to do this?" Runner asked, his voice low.

"You haven't given me a choice," I replied watching Texas swirl the glass, mixing the drug. "You want your dickhead of a President gone. I want to make sure no women are ever hurt again."

Texas held out the glass to me. "It's ready, just drink it straight down."

"What is it?"

"Rohypnol."

Loss of muscle control, confusion, drowsiness, and temporary amnesia.

The downside to being a biochemist—I had an unholy fascination with understanding side effects. "You're sure this is what they use?"

"Yeah, Mouse stole the pills."

Fuck.

Hands settled on my shoulders giving me a squeeze.

"You don't have to do this," Ava whispered. "We can work out something else."

I sucked in a breath then took the glass from Texas.

"You've got my back," I told her. "I trust you."

And as hard as it was to admit, I somehow trusted these men around me. Perhaps it was the fact they hadn't tried to take the weapons from Ava or I. Or maybe it was the way they looked so... remorseful? Ashamed?

No, desperate. That's what it was. *Desperation.*

I tipped the glass back, downing the mix, shuddering as the alcohol hit my throat, burning as it slid down to pool in my stomach.

"What now?" Ava asked.

"We wait," I replied, coughing at the burn. I leaned forward placing the now empty glass on Texas's coffee table. "Shouldn't take long."

I stayed seated for all of thirty seconds, then got up to pace, muttering, "Could you all just... do something please? I can't deal with you staring at me."

They moved, Texas busying himself with the lockbox and Ava tidying up the kitchen.

The only one who remained watching me was Runner.

"What?" I asked, continuing to pace.

"Gotta get our story straight." He jerked his head at Texas, who was pretending to dust his book shelf. "He found you and sent for me. Got it?"

I nodded, the movement sending my head spinning.

"Shit," I muttered, stopping to raise a hand to my head. "Looks like it's working."

"Won't be long now," Runner muttered, crossing the room to lay hands on my shoulders. "Sit, Baby Girl."

My butt hit the couch as my stomach rolled in protest, my world beginning to spin.

"We'll take you to Church and call Butcher and your sister. They'll be able to verify the drug in your system."

"Butcher?" Ava asked, having given up cleaning.

"Doctor," Texas answered.

"Two verifications, smart," she muttered.

"What about Mouse?" I asked. Or at least, I tried to. The words came out wrong, mangled, and slurred, my mouth no longer responding to my directions.

"Mouse?" Runner asked, somehow clarifying my question.

I tried to nod but found my head slumping to the side instead, my body slowly relaxing into the cushions.

"She's good. She knows what to do," Texas answered.

"You sure?"

"Positive."

"Mouse?" Ava asked.

"Tell you later," Texas replied as Runner squatted before me, his hand reaching to lift my head a fraction.

"I'm gonna pick you and take you to Church. You cool with that?"

I raised my head a fraction. "Okay."

Runner nodded, squeezed my knee then stood, bending to shift me around and lift me. He held me close to his chest, as one would a bride.

"Ava, guns up, look fierce. Texas, same. Get Pope to raise the alarm. I want Beast to find Butcher and Ellie's sister. Ghost'll

89

be out there if Ava's here. Get him round to my place. See if we can't intercept Gus trying to find Ellie. If we're lucky he'll have broken into my apartment and Ghost can really fuck him up. We'll meet everyone at Church."

He pulled me closer, tucking my head against his shoulder. "Let's go."

Chapter Fourteen

Runner

I sat in my designated spot at the long table, Ellie cradled against my chest. My brothers trickled in, each staring at the drooling, barely conscious woman in my arms as they took their seats or stood, backs pressed against the concrete wall of the Club House

It took a while for them all to arrive, one by one summoned by Pope.

The silence in the room was deafening.

On one side of me stood Ava, guns on either hip, arms crossed, glaring at every man who walked through the door. On my other stood Texas, casually cleaning his pistol. This put my brothers on edge—weapons, except in anything but the most extraordinary of circumstances, were a clear violation of the sanctity of Church.

"Where is she!" A feminine voice demanded.

"The sister's here," Texas muttered.

Blair burst into the sanctuary, her hair wild, her eyes wide, Butcher hot on her heels. She spotted Ellie and immediately came to us, her hands going to Ellie's cheeks, gently tilting her head back to examine her. She pulled a small torch from her pocket, shining it in Ellie's eyes.

"Muscle control loss, dilated pupils," Blair murmured, feeling for Ellie's pulse. "Sluggish."

"Drugged," Butcher said crossing his arms and lifting an eyebrow at me. "Your girl's been drugged, Runner."

Blair shot to standing, a hand coming up to slap me. "You fucking bastard!"

Texas stepped in, catching her hand mid-swipe. "No, babe. He didn't do it."

Blair paused, looking to Ava for confirmation. Ava nodded once, then jerked her head at the door.

"Hold tight, the main attraction's here."

Pope and Beast entered, followed closely by the Prez and Mama, their cheeks flushed and angry. Ghost trailed guns pointed to their backs, Mouse bringing up the rear, closing the door behind her.

"What the fuck are ye thinkin'?" Prez demanded, looking around the room. "Who the fuck do ye pissants think ye are?"

"Sit down," I ordered, shifting Ellie closer. Pope and Beast came to stand behind me, guns trained on Mama and Prez. Ghost moved to Ava's side on the other end of the table, ignoring his seat, choosing to remain standing.She raised an eyebrow at him but his focus was solely on the Prez.

Gus hesitated, gauging the atmosphere in the room. Finally, stiffly, he sat, taking up his position at the top of the round table.

Not for long.

"Explain," he said stiffly.

"Church is in session, and hold, Gus," I told him, my tone filled with icy rage. "A reckoning is upon us."

He glared at me; his mouth pressed into a thin, furious line.

"Texas?" I prompted, watching the Prez.

"Stumbled across Mouse leading Ellie here back to Runner's apartment. Only, Ellie wasn't moving so good. Ain't that, right Mouse?"

Mouse nodded, her shoulders hunched, her face turned away from the group. She clutched a battered notebook in her arms. "Ellie kept falling and I wasn't strong enough to pick her up."

"So, she's sick," Prez rolled his eyes. "Big deal."

"No," Blair interrupted, throwing an arm out to point at her sister. "Anyone with half a fucking brain can see my sister has been drugged. She can't even raise her fucking head."

Prez rubbed his chin, his eyes narrowing. "And ye think this has something to do with me?"

"I think it has everything to do with you," I replied easily. "My woman walked off with you. She went straight to visit with Mama. Next time I see her she's in this state."

"Bullshit," Prez barked. "Coulda been anything."

"But it wasn't, was it?" I asked coldly. "Mama?"

The woman stood behind the Prez, her arms crossed, her expression stubborn. "Ain't got nothing to do with me."

"Liar."

All heads twisted to see Mouse staring at the woman, her expression mutinous. "Ellie is the fifteenth woman you've drugged." She slapped the notebook down on the table. "I've recorded them. I know where you store your little stash of drugs. You drug these women then decide what you want to do with them. Some are kept here, like Wendy. Convinced they just drank too much, or threatened so they'll fall in line. But the others are sent to God knows where." She sucked in a breath. "You're a monster."

The brothers moved at this revelation, some yelling protests, some making threats. The men at my back remained still, all their concentration on the Prez.

He slapped a gavel down, calling the rabble to order. It took a few tries before the gathered men quietened, watching through narrowed eyes.

Prez considered me. "Never took ye for a mutineer, Runner."

"Never took you for a fucking liar," I returned.

"You're gonna take the word of a fucking woman over your brother?" Gus asked the table.

"Ghost, where did you pick them up?" I asked, not breaking eye contact with Gus. His gaze flickered, his confidence dimming for a split second.

"Your apartment," Ghost rumbled, his voice like gravel. "They had this with 'em." He pulled a pack from his shoulder tossing it on the table. Chief, our Vice President, reached for it, pulling out rope, a blindfold, cable ties, and a rag that could be used to gag a person.

The table fell silent. Divine judgement was about to be visited upon the Prez.

Gus read the room, his body stiffening. He leaned back in this chair, knitting his fingers together, considering each of us in turn. Perhaps he was looking for loyalty. Perhaps he thought he would find mercy or forgiveness.

The man would find nothing but retribution in this room. He'd broken faith with his brotherhood.

"What do ye want?" Prez finally asked.

"You gone. Your woman gone. You ever show your fucking faces here again and I'll kill you myself."

Prez raised an eyebrow. "Ye'd do that over some gash?"

Rage roared through me, fury igniting my veins, setting my

body aflame.

"This woman is mine. But she's also the club's. Ellie knows how to make fuel so we can ride free. Her knowledge will help our brothers in other chapters. When our nomad brothers come, she can teach them and they can take it back to others. She is our fucking salvation and you wanted to do... what? Sell her to The Purge? Hand her over to someone for some fucking cash?" I spat on the table. "You're a fucking disgrace. A traitor. You don't deserve to wear the kutte on your back or occupy the seat of the great presidents who came before you."

"Ye have no idea what the fuck ye're talking about!" Gus broke, slamming both fists on the table and surging to his feet. "Everything I fucking do is for this club! Ye think we live here by the fucking grace of God? Ye're a goddamned fool."

He spun looking at the brothers around him. "The girls I send to The Purge and the goddamned Rivals? That's what keeps ye here. Ye and ye offspring and ye fucking women. Not ye brawn and ye fucking guns. Me!" He stabbed a finger into his chest. "I'm ye fucking saviour. Not some bitch who can conjure a fucking thimble of fuel."

"So, you admit it?" Chief asked. "You've sold women before?"

"Oh, get off ye fucking high horse," Prez scoffed. "Ye'd all be long dead if not for me."

"Why did they want *this* girl though?" Chief asked, getting to his feet, and crossing his arms over his chest. "Was it her knowledge? And how did they even know about her?"

"'Cause I fucking told them. They want fuel. And pussy. Two in one deal. Were gonna give us a reprieve for twelve months if I provided her to them. Any other woman we could keep." He glanced at Ellie, his lips pulling into a sneer. "Just me luck she had to go get herself fucked by the first randy boyo to throw her a look."

And thank God she did.

"Vote, brothers." Chief looked around the room. "All those in favour of excommunicating Prez and his woman say aye."

"Aye," the unanimous voices heralded.

"Seems you'll find no support here, Gus," Chief leaned in. "Someone remove this fucking piece of shit and his woman from my sight. And make sure you strip his kutte and burn it."

"With pleasure," answered Hazard, our Enforcer. He slapped a hand on Gus' shoulder. "Come on, old man, you got a long journey ahead of you."

He frog-marched the protesting Gus from the room, Ice pulling a wailing Mama behind them. Two of the soldiers peeled off, following to lend support. The door shut and all eyes went to Chief.

"We'll call for nominations today, put it to a vote in two days," he declared, running a hand over his face. "Need a volunteer to send word to the other chapters. Can't have Gus out running his mouth."

"I got it," Whip said, pushing up from the table. "I'll go once the girl is good. And I'll let the chapters know that fuel is on its way."

Chief nodded. "Good thinking. Anything else?"

"Gus' women and Mouse," Texas asked. "Whatcha gonna do with them?"

Chief looked to Ava. "You want to take on a few more in the Hen House?"

"Hen House?" she asked, quirking one eyebrow.

"You can call it whatever you want as long as you keep your women in line." Chief slapped a closed fist to his chest. "We vowed to keep you safe. The man who led that vow broke it.

We're setting it right."

"He broke it and yet you're letting him live," Ava said mildly. "Seems like a pretty shitty way to set something right."

"Don't think they'll be getting off lightly, girl. Gus and Mama will be stripped naked and blindfolded. Then they'll be driven hours from here to the top of a mountain and dumped. They'll remain blindfolded and naked, tied to a tree within hearing distance of each other but not within touch. They won't be given any clothing, food, or water. No guns or knives. They'll be left there for whoever has mercy on them—be it God or man."

Ava considered the VP. "Still think you should put a bullet in him. My experience is rats always find a way to escape." She shrugged. "But that sounds like an acceptable second option."

The air lightened as the men around us chuckled.

"Are we good?" Blair asked, reaching a hand down to check Ellie's pulse again. "I'd like to take her to the infirmary and get some fluids into her. It won't help the drugs, but it'll help the hangover."

"Any last thoughts?" Chief asked, looking from one brother to the next until he was sure they were all satisfied. "Dismissed."

Chapter Fifteen

Ellie

The pounding in my head woke me.

"Christ," I groaned, eyes screwed shut. "I'm dying."

"No, just a really horrible hangover." My sister's hand brushed hair from my sweaty forehead. "You can have some painkillers in a second. You need to eat something first or you'll just throw it back up."

I forced my eyes open and found myself in a hospital-like room. Though, it felt more like one of the makeshift clinics that had been set up in the before, when the virus had first begun its rapid spread.

"Where am I?"

"This is their infirmary." Blair snorted, fluffing the pillow behind me. "Let's just say I have my work cut out for me."

Butcher entered the room, a plate in one hand, a cup of something steaming in the other.

"Here." He placed it on the bedside table. "Toast first, have a little tea then we'll get the painkillers into you."

I accepted the offered toast, nibbling on a corner as my stomach rolled in protest.

Quiet you.

Butcher was... not what I expected. Average height but with above-average looks, he struck me as a good old boy, the kind you'd take home to momma. Definitely not the type to join a motorcycle club.

He wore a worn, plain black shirt and jeans, his dark hair in need of a cut but not overly unruly. He was clean shaven—an unusual occurrence in this land of the hairy.

"Why do they call you Butcher?" I asked, sipping at the weak but sugary tea.

"Had to cut off a man's leg once at a roadside accident. The name stuck."

I swallowed. "Sorry I asked."

He grinned, revealing a set of white, perfectly straight teeth.

"You definitely don't look like a gang member."

"We're not a gang," he corrected, moving to the bedside table, and pulling out some painkillers from one of the drawers. "We're a club. It's like family."

"You don't look like a club member, then," I corrected. I held out my hand, accepting the painkillers Butcher popped out into my hand. He passed me a glass of water and I swallowed, grimacing at the taste.

"It's the lack of hair, right?" He rubbed a hand across his face. "Hair in wounds isn't advisable so I keep it tight." He winked. "Besides, who would cover up sheer perfection?"

Blair snorted from across the room where she was sorting vials. "High opinion of yourself."

"Baby, you think this face is pretty you should see my d—"

"You're awake."

I shivered, watching Runner as he stalked across the room to my side. He looked exhausted, dark circles bruised the skin under his eyes, his mouth pressed into a thin line, hair standing on end.

"You need sleep."

He ignored my statement, coming to cup my face in his big hands. "You good?"

I shrugged. "Head feels like it's about to explode but I'll live."

"The painkillers will kick in shortly. She needs to sleep. We'll continue the fluids for another cycle but by that stage she'll be good to go home," Butcher commented, checking the IV line.

"And by home, he means to the Hen House." My sister replied, crossing her arms over her ample chest, and glaring at Runner. "*Not* with you."

Runner ignored Blair, his gaze like a caress as he examined me. "You wanna come home with me?"

I hesitated.

No. Yes. Maybe. I don't know. Yes.

"Not today," I said, looking away. "I need time."

His lips pressed together into a displeased line. "How much time?"

"I don't know." I shrugged. "Enough to feel safe again."

"And you don't with me?"

"Not today."

He pulled back, running a hand through his hair. "Right." He turned on his heel, heading for the door. "I'll get your things moved."

And with that he left. The pounding in my head took second place to the ache in my chest.

"Good girl," Blair said, squeezing my shoulder. "You can't trust him."

Can't I? My heart asked.

I sighed, closing my eyes, exhaustion overriding my sense,

turning my limbs to heavy weights. "Gonna sleep now."

"You do that, babe." My sister whispered, stroking a cool hand over my brow. "I'll be right here, keeping you safe."

Safe.

In this strange after time, what was safe anymore? The only time I'd felt safe in months had been in Runner's bed as he forced me to cede all control, all worries, all concerns to him. He'd lifted the burden of being strong and just let me be.

And in one afternoon that had shattered.

Sleep first. We can work this out later.

I gave in, letting the darkness enclose, finding an elusive slice of peace in the unconscious.

Chapter Sixteen

Runner

"You're wallowing."

I ignored Hazard's statement, instead asking, "It's done?"

He slid onto the bar stool beside me, leaning on the bar and jerking his head at a prospect. "Give us a beer, would you?"

The kid slid a perfectly poured glass in front of Hazard. He took a long drink, setting it down on the wooden bar counter.

When our founders had bought this place, the first thing they'd done was transform the main hall into a proper bar, complete with fridges, keg taps, and enough hard stuff to last the apocalypse. A few years back, some entrepreneurial brother had set up a homebrew station in one of the sheds, creating liquors, whiskeys, and ciders that—if not great—were at least passable for alcohol. *Thank God for them.* I toasted silently, nursing my whiskey.

The hall itself was filled with lounges, pool tables, and a few tables. Years ago, someone had gotten it into their mind to bump the back of the hall out. The brothers had all pitched in, installing giant bi-fold doors that opened onto a massive deck with an outdoor grilling/smoking set-up, that led down to a cleared grass area complete with big-arse fire pit.

In the before we'd spent weekends partying out there, cooking and carousing. Tonight, the doors were closed, the mood inside sombre.

Tomorrow we'd vote on who will take over our club. I'd assumed Chief but the man wasn't interested, satisfied with his VP position, and the younger brothers were murmuring of needing new blood in this time of uncertainty.

Either way, it's a change.

"It's done," Hazard finally said, drawing my attention back. "Dumped him and the missus, got them situated and drove back. Makes you feel better, we made them walk up a fucking mountain in the fucking dark with no shoes so they'd no idea where the road is."

"Should've listened to Ava, put a bullet in him," I muttered, signalling the prospect acting as the bartender for tonight for a refill.

"You mean Legs?" Hazard tilted his head down the far side of the bar where Ava sat nursing a beer. She'd obviously been working out earlier, her legs on display thanks to a pair of tiny jogging shorts.

"Mm."

Hazard ran a hand across his face. "She like men?"

"How the fuck would I know?"

"Your girl didn't mention it?"

Resentment sat in my stomach, poisoning my mood. "I had her for one fucking night. You think we spent that time having pillow chats?"

Hazard chuckled. "See? You're wallowing." He slapped a hand on my back. "Man up, dude. You want your woman? Go fucking win her." He pushed away from the bar. "Now,

I'm gonna go try my luck with Legs. See you at the vote tomorrow." He turned then paused. "And maybe while you're over at the Hen House you could see to inviting them women to our cookout? Gonna be a big night, don't want our newest members to miss out."

I grunted, lifting my glass, and letting the whiskey burn its way back down my throat.

Go fucking win her.

Maybe it was Hazard's encouragement or the whiskey but an idea took root. A fucking crazy one, but an idea that somehow, in this moment, seemed fucking brilliant.

Go win her.

I left the bar, passing Ghost who was once again seated in the shadows, his eyes on Ava and Hazard.

He glanced at me, giving me a chin lift, before looking back at the couple, his face carved from stone.

Poor bastard.

Hunching my shoulders against the cool night air, I headed for the mess hall. A single light was on in the kitchen, the sound of soft chatter filtering into the dining room.

"Yo," I called, not wanting to startle anyone.

A head poked out over the bain-maries.

"Runner, right?" the girl with long black hair asked.

"Yeah, can I come in?"

"Free country," she said, ducking back into the kitchen.

I walked through the doors, finding a production line in progress.

"Shit, what's this?"

"Croissants, pain au chocolat, and custard Danishes." The woman waved her hand at the thousands of pastries. "You guys had all the fixings. I couldn't help myself."

104

My mouth watered just looking at the unbaked goods. "You're a baker?"

"Chef." She held out a hand, then dropped it, dusting it off against her apron before holding it out again. "Sorry, I'm Yana."

I shook her hand then glanced around. "Just you in here? I thought I heard voices."

"Oh." She blushed. "I talk to the pastry. It makes them tastier."

I'd heard of people talking to plants and animals before, but never food.

"Whatever works for you," I said with a shrug. "I actually wanted to steal some cocoa."

"For?"

I swallowed. "Gotta make something."

"Hot cocoa or baking?"

"Baking. Brownies."

Yana's face split into a massive grin. "For you or someone else?"

I shoved my hands into my jean pockets. "What's with the interrogation? You got cocoa or not?"

"Right, so they're for Ellie." She turned, moving to a door at the rear of the kitchen. "I have a mass of cocoa. I'll give credit to you guys; you know how to prep like mofos. This place is a goddamned dream."

She disappeared and I heard movement, some scraping and then a muttered curse. A moment later she reappeared, holding a small cannister out to me.

"If you want, I have fresh eggs, milk and I just made some butter. I also have freeze-dried raspberries which would go perfectly with those brownies."

I raised an eyebrow. "Where'd you get milk from? And the berries?"

"We brought cows with us, duh." She rolled her eyes, patting the bench beside her. "And we grew the berries and I preserved them. I'm a zombie-chef-er."

"A... a what?"

"You know, a woman ready for the apocalypse?" She sighed, "Come on, lover boy. Let me teach you my ways."

Under her tutelage I created a massive pan of thick, gooey chocolate brownies with delicious raspberries sprinkled across the top.

"Perfect," Yana declared, dusting her hands. "And on that note, you should deliver these tonight while you still have time."

I glanced at the clock, frowning. "Will she be awake?"

"Honey, even if she isn't, she'll want to be for these." She leaned over swiping a small square from the top of the container, moaning as she bit into it.

"It's been over a year since we had chocolate. A year, Runner. Do you know what that does to a woman?"

I rolled my eyes, lifting the heavy container. "Wish me luck."

"Buddy, you don't need luck. You got chocolate. But come back when you're done. I'll need that container back."

"You need a hand with this?" I asked, gesturing at the half-baked pastries.

"Nah." She waved me off. "This'll be one more batch then I'll be headed to bed. I've got a prospect and one of the girls running the breakfast shift tomorrow." She smiled. "Thanks though. If it helps, I think you're alright. Which is all we can really ask for in the after."

I huffed out a laugh. "Thanks, catch you tomorrow."

"Remember the container!"

I left the warmth of the kitchen, making a mental note to

go find some extra blankets for Ellie. We may be in the midst of Spring, but the nights here were still cool, and tonight felt particularly chilly.

The Hen House sat off to the far side of the main building cluster. I clocked Jo before I got there. She was hip deep in the engine bay of a truck parked beside the barracks.

"Need a hand?" I asked.

She shot me a look over her shoulder then sniffed, looking back into the bay that was lit by a solitary torch.

I sighed, "I'm sorry. We should have told you."

Jo ignored me, loudly banging a wrench against the engine mounts.

I'm not above bribery.

"I brought brownies."

The banging paused. "Chocolate?"

"And raspberry," I confirmed, holding the container up and giving it a gentle shake. "Yana approved."

She straightened, jumping off the front bumper and sliding hands over her overalls. "Well, hand it over then."

I pulled one free, offering it to her on a napkin Yana had helpfully included. Jo took one bite then moaned as if I'd given her an orgasm.

"Forgiven," she declared around a bite. "They're warm, gooey and chocolatey. You bring me another batch next week and you can have whatever the fuck you want."

I grinned. "Am I allowed in to see Ellie?"

She waved a hand off toward the entrance. "Go with my blessing, good sir."

I found the women clustered in the main sitting area on the bottom floor of the barracks. They had an array of tubes and jars strewn about, and multi-coloured gunk slathered across their faces and limbs, and a few with it in their hair. In the middle, sat Ellie. Her eyes widening as she clocked me.

"I brought you brownies," I said, holding up the container lamely.

This was a fucking stupid idea.

"Brownies?" Audrey asked from her seat on the floor. She too had stuff smeared across her face, but instead of jars and tubes, she was surrounded by electronic parts and tiny tools.

"Uh, yeah." I held out the box, offering it to Ellie. "It's an apology. For being shitty."

"They're good too," Jo sang, entering behind me and side stepping the mess to sit on the one empty spot on the couch. "Gooey and a little warm."

The ravenous horde descended but I lifted the treats, holding them out of reach of the grasping hands. "Uh-uh," I tutted. "These are Ellie's."

The sea of women parted, and Ellie slowly stepped forward. Despite the pink shade of goo on her face, she was still the most beautiful woman in the room.

"Thank you," she said, accepting the box. "This is very kind."

"Very kind?" A woman I'd not yet met repeated, one hand propping on her hip. "Girl, the man baked. And he baked chocolate. *Chocolate*. Hell, I couldn't even get a man to do that for me in the before. But in the after? Where the hell does one even find cocoa?"

There were general murmurings of agreement.

"Doesn't change the fact he didn't warn us about the drugging," Blair pointed out.

"True," another woman returned. "But it goes a little bit of the way to making us want to forgive him though, right?"

The group seemed split.

"I didn't see this," Audrey said, tilting her head to the side as she frowned at me.

"See what?" I asked, shoving now empty hands into my pockets in an attempt to keep from reaching for Ellie.

"You. Brownies. Baking." She shook her head. "Didn't predict this. Wasn't in the scenarios."

I glanced at Ellie, lifting an eyebrow in question. She shrugged.

"I'd argue your scenarios need more data," one girl commented.

Audrey seemed to consider this. "Actually, you are correct." She narrowed her gaze on me. "When can I set up interviews with the men?"

"Huh?"

She made an impatient wave of her hand. "I need more data. If I have enough data on an individual, I can predict within a two percent margin their behaviours and actions towards certain stimuli. It's been immensely helpful during this period."

"You could have predicted I'd bake brownies?"

She shrugged. "Potentially. I had you at five-to-one odds of arriving here tonight. And there is a higher percentage that you wouldn't have left without Ellie. Though I'd argue that you not leaving is more about you deciding to camp here until she either forgives you or you're satisfied we're safe rather than you forcing her back to your apartment."

I mean... she's not wrong.

I scrubbed a hand over my face. "I'm not sure I completely understand what's happening right now."

"Don't worry," a girl said from my side. "We all feel like that when talking to Audrey."

It wasn't reassuring.

I looked back at Ellie. "There's a cookout tomorrow night, after the vote. You guys are all invited of course. But… can I take you?"

Ellie blinked. "Like a date?"

"Sure."

The girls around the room immediately tittered. I caught sight of Mouse at the back, she rolled her eyes then immediately buried her head back in the book she was reading.

Ellie considered me; her arms wrapped around the container. "On one condition."

I gritted my teeth. "Name it."

"You can't sleep with me."

Fuck.

It wasn't that I wanted my dick wet, though I'd fucking love to be balls deep inside Ellie's tight little pussy. No, it was that I wanted to give her the release she so desperately needed.

It hadn't escaped my notice that she'd come to me with a fuckload of tension and stress written across every line in her body. It also hadn't escaped my notice that I'd managed to erase some of it by taking control, by getting her to submit, by bringing her pleasure.

Give me enough time and a bed and I can take the rest too.

"No penetration," I agreed.

"Thank—"

"Unless you want it." I interrupted.

Ellie frowned. "That's not gonna happen."

"Good, then you shouldn't have an issue with that condition."

She blew out a breath. " I'll see you tomorrow night."

"Can't wait."

Chapter Seventeen

Ellie

I sipped the craft beer Runner had gotten for me, watching the festivities. He'd disappeared to get us some food and left me sitting by the giant fire pit. Around me, men spoke, toasting their new President, Hazard, and his VP, Chief. They also had a new Enforcer, Nails, so named because apparently, he was sharp as a tack.

Look, I didn't get the name thing but I went with it.

The new Prez was drinking slowly, looking a little serious for all the revelry around him. But he accepted congratulations and drink top-ups.

"He didn't want it," Runner remarked, materialising beside me balancing two plates.

"Want what?"

"The position. Didn't wanna be Prez."

"Why not? Why'd he take it then?"

"Thinks he'll suck at it, the rest of us don't have any concerns. And you don't turn down that kind of opportunity."

He handed me a plate piled with food. Smoked ribs, barbequed chicken wings, fresh bread rolls, coupled with a heaping of mac and cheese, some kind of bean mix, a corn cob, and fresh potato salad.

"Wow, you guys know how to put on a party," I remarked, reaching for the ribs.

"Thank your friend. Normally it's just meat and whatever the ladies have scraped together. This is the best fucking food we've had since the local pizza place shut down."

I chuckled, biting into the succulent piece of meat, and groaning as the juicy and smoky flavour burst across my tongue.

"Yana deserves a medal."

"No complaining from this side."

We shared a grin then went back to devouring the delicious feast. Yana was never happier than when she was feeding our motley crew. With the increased food selection, and oh so appreciative diners she was sure to be in seventh heaven.

"Honestly, this morning it almost felt like the before," Runner commented scooping up a mouthful of the bean salad. "Those pastries were next level."

I felt a pang in my gut. "Unless we get seeds and start regulating our breeding meat stock, we probably won't be eating like this regularly."

Runner chewed, considering my comment. "What kind of seeds?"

I shrugged. "Well for cocoa we'd need plants since the seeds spoil quickly so can't be dried."

Runner raised his eyebrows in question.

"Kate," I explained. "She's our botanist and expert on all things plants."

"And you've spoken about this before?"

"Chocolate and coffee," I explained, as if that answered

everything.

"You could grow coffee here?"

"I wish." I shook my head. "It needs a tropical climate. Unless you guys have the power to reproduce one in one of those sheds and maintain that year-round, no."

"Damn," he licked his fingers. "Guess we need to talk to some brothers up north, set up a trading pipeline."

"You could do that?"

"Sure," Runner said, shrugging. "If the government ain't gonna provide for us, and big business has shat itself, our next best option is to do it ourselves."

"What did you do in the before?" I asked, putting my plate on the ground, and beginning to clean my hands with a napkin.

"Accountant. I did the books for the club."

A stuttering laugh exploded from my mouth. I slapped a hand to my lips, horrified. "Sorry!"

"Eh, don't be," he said, offering me a twisted grin. "I know I don't look like an accountant but fact is, I'm good with numbers."

I couldn't help but take him in. The lean, muscular body with tattoos that ran down each arm. His strong legs and attractive mouth, his broad chest and mop of unruly hair. Not to mention his filthy mouth and dominating presence in bed.

Yeah, definitely doesn't look like any accountant I know.

I would have enjoyed doing my taxes if he'd been sitting across the desk.

"What do you do now?"

"Still run the treasury, but now it's more like wrangling timesheets and counting barrels of food trying to find a middle ground than it is balancing spreadsheets."

"I don't understand."

He placed his empty plate beside mine then reached for a stick, scratching a two-sided table in the dirt. I could just make it out in the fire light.

"In the before, the men payed their dues to the club, worked at one of our businesses or substituted either of the first two by doing extra duties, like patrols or running shit from one chapter to another."

I nodded my understanding.

"In the after, it ain't that easy. Everyone needs to work together to contribute. So, I divide the tasks. We got some guys who have specialised skills, like Butcher or Ghost. Doctors, farmers, plumbers. Whatever."

He marked two scratches in the first column. "But the majority of our guys were truck drivers or ran our businesses, so they need to pivot and do other things. To encourage them to do that, I set a quota each month. Something like ten bags of corn picked, or three nights out on patrol." He flashed me a smile. "Most of the time, unless we're told by our experts there's a deadline, I don't much care how long it takes them to do their duties. As long as it gets done that's the main thing."

"And what do they get it they complete this?"

"Well, nothing if they complete it. But if they don't meet it for any reason other than sickness, which Butcher has to sign off on, then they get additional duties. And the duties are shit. Things like pumping the sewage tanks and driving it out to the old quarry to dump it. Or cleaning the barn, or washing. Shit no one wants."

"And what if they get it all done? Who does those tasks?

"Then those jobs go to the prospects."

Runner gestured towards the front of the compound. "There are a few guys on watch tonight, but most of the guards are prospects. They've gotta prove themselves somehow."

"Where do they come from?"

"Some of them were with us from other chapters since the before. You don't prospect where your family is. We don't do favouritism in the Nameless Souls."

I nodded, it made sense.

"But for the rest? Some were here before shit went down. Some came as it happened, others joined in the months since." He shrugged. "We occasionally get a kid who wanders upon us, and we take 'em in. Some stick around. Some leave. Up to them."

"Don't you worry about them revealing your location?"

"Sure. But you can't worry about what you can't change. Unless you're planning on moving every few months you gotta stick around, fortify what you own, defend it."

He looked around then nodded towards a guy with dark brown hair. He stood off to the side of the party, his back to the brick wall of the Club House. Half his face remained in shadow as he quietly watched the world party around him.

"That's Ghost, our Warlord. He's in charge of security. Went to war before this shit went down. Rumour has it some kind of special forces guy. Either way, the man is dead inside. We called him Ghost because he is one. Completely. You'd never see or hear him coming. He wants you dead? You're knocking on the reapers door letting him know it's time."

I shivered. "So, you're pretty confident you guys can keep this place safe?"

"Hundred percent."

I took some comfort in that.

The music started up again, a cheer rising from those gathered around the fire. One of the older guys came over, sitting beside Runner and making small talk. Runner slung an arm around me, keeping me close as he chatted, shooting the breeze.

A group of women, some of them I recognized, some I didn't, began to dance at the front of the stage, singing and laughing. Beth joined them, twirling, and singing along.

This all felt strangely... normal. Despite us living well back at the College, we'd had to live meagre and secretive lives. There had been security shifts every night, chores every day. We'd each had jobs to do and we'd worked to do them. But the fear, anxiety and general sense of exhaustion hadn't left a lot of space for laughter or relaxation. There'd been no singing or dancing. No cookouts or nights like this, with a big bonfire and beer.

We'd done well, worked hard, kept ourselves safe. But this was a slice of normality. A gift of feeling like we were...

Home?

I pushed the thought away, choosing to ignore it for the moment and instead concentrate on the now.

A prospect brought us another round of beers; Yana produced marshmallows and corn kernels to cook over the fire, the popcorn, and gooey sweets freely shared

As the night wore on, the crowd became a little rowdier, and kids were whisked off to bed. Couples settled in, a few getting particularly grabby with PDAs. But I didn't mind. Tonight felt like a reprieve from the humdrum of monotonous survival.

Runner pulled me in, whispering in my ear, "Pope's gonna make his move."

I looked to the stage, seeing him eyeing off Beth. She danced at the front, singing along to a punk-rock version of "Faith" by George Michael. Her cheeks were flushed, and her body moved with the fluidity of a woman who was at least a little tipsy.

They finished the song and Pope reached down, gesturing for Beth to take his hand, and come on stage. Beth hesitated for a moment, her cheeks flushing bright red, but she took his hand, allowing him to pull her up. She teetered for a moment but he steadied her, hands settling on her waist.

I glanced at Jo who stood near me. Her face was frozen, her expression hopeful as she watched her younger sister.

Beth leaned closer to Pope, whispering something in his ear. He laughed, looked at her serious expression then shrugged. He took the microphone handed it to her then began to strum the hauntingly familiar chords of "Hallelujah." The crowd quietened, all eyes going to the stage.

Beth hesitated for a moment, glancing at the crowd, then she turned her back on us, instead swaying in time to the music.

"Go, Beth," I whispered, sending her strength.

Her shoulders drew back then her glorious voice floated out over the speakers.

Beth swayed, her back still to us as she sang about beauty and moonlight. Around us, the world fell silent, bikers and women listening to the most heartfelt rendition of this song we'd likely ever heard. This was a time where we'd killed people, where we'd been forced to make sacrifices and decisions that allowed us to survive. We'd been cold. We'd been broken. We'd prayed, asking for forgiveness, for guidance, for love. In this moment, the song took on a deeper meaning. And everyone around me could feel it.

"Hallelujah," Beth sang, her voice soulful, mournful, her essence in every word, every chord, every note.

Runner's arms wrapped around my middle, pulling me close.

Tears soaked my cheeks as Pope played and Beth sang, and the audience listened to a broken woman begging for salvation.

She ended on a trembling note, a beat of silence following.

I looked to Jo, finding her and Ruby clutching each other, tears streaming down their faces.

Applause started slowly, as if we were scared that even that minor vibration would shatter the woman before us. But it swelled, and soon the bikers and women were roaring and stamping our approval.

Pope broke into a grin, his voice just barely audible through the microphone. "Fucking-A, girl. You can sing."

Beth turned, her cheeks flushed, eyes bright.

"More!" I shouted, and the chant was taken up.

"Choose something up beat this time," Pope said. "My heart can't take another like that."

Beth bit her lower lip, then bent down again, whispering something once again into Pope's ear. He grinned and began to strum.

"'Time after time'?" Ava asked, appearing beside me, a drink in her hand. "Beth needs some new material."

I laughed, sinking into Runner. "It's a classic."

"If you say so." She lifted the beer cup to her lips, tilting her head to eye Runner with a sly grin. "You should go dance with the girls, Ellie. Maybe take Runner with you. "

I shot her a glare but Runner chuckled behind me, his chest rumbling against my back. "Great idea."

"What?" I barked, surprised.

He dropped his hands, pulling me onto the dance floor. It was little more than a cleared dirt patch in front of the makeshift stage. A few women were laughing, swaying, and singing to each other. They cleared a space for Runner to pull me close.

He fit me into his arms, pressing me close to him swaying us in time to the music.

"Aren't you afraid of your brothers making fun?" I asked, laughing as he spun me out and then slowly twirled me back into him.

"Nope, they get it."

"Get what?"

"You do what you gotta do for your woman." He dipped me, grinning as he held me suspended for a moment. "And dancing gets you wet."

"How do you know that?" I asked breathless, my hair flowing down to the ground.

"I didn't. Do now though." He pulled me back up, setting us back to a steady sway.

I caught Beth's eye as she sang. She sent me a little wave and a smile as she continued to sing.

Runner pressed his forehead to mine. I got lost in the green of his eyes, the warmth of his hand clasping mine, the press of his chest against me. I wanted to let go, to let him take control, to let him lead me to the same sweet release.

The song finished and we stepped back to clap, Pope immediately jumping into "Bad Moon Rising."

Runner took my hand, pulling me into him. He leaned in, his lips grazing the shell of my ear as he whispered, "You wanna dance more or get a drink?"

"I want you to take me to bed," I answered.

He stiffened. "You sure?"

I pulled back, arching an eyebrow at him. "You're really gonna look a gift horse in the mou—"

He picked me up, slinging me over his shoulder in a fireman hold and took off towards the barracks.

I laughed, waving at Ava, Jo and Ruby as we passed.

"Get it girl!" Ruby yelled, lifting her glass in toast.

We moved through the crowd and the last thing I heard was Audrey yelling at me to take notes.

"We want details!"

"Your friends are nuts," Runner remarked, hurrying through the dark towards his apartment.

"Says the man who throws me over his shoulder every five minutes." I reached down, patting his arse. "You need to watch it, you'll put your back out. I'm heavy."

"So, help me God, if you even think about losing one pound, I'll take you over my knee and spank you," he threatened, one hand going up to cup my arse. "I like your curves far too much, Baby Girl."

Oh, he can have whatever he wants. I mean, maybe not anal. But I'd at least consider it.

Chapter Eighteen

Runner

I laid Ellie down on the bed, pausing for a moment to kiss her, then pulled back.

"Where are you going?" she asked, watching me as I moved to my chest of drawers.

"Strip, Baby Girl." I pulled a drawer open, digging through the depths to pull a length of rope free. I looped it around my hand, enjoying the feel of the bamboo fibres as it glided across my palm.

"Ready, Runner," my girl said from behind me.

I grinned, remaining in place. "Get on all fours, head away from me."

I heard her move, settling on the bed. Her voice held a tremor as she called, "Done."

I turned then, taking a moment to admire the view. When I was out on runs, I occasionally saw women. It'd been less than a year since the world went dark completely, but already there was a sharpness about the women I saw. Their bodies thinner, their faces hollower, a hardness to them that didn't sit right in my gut.

Ellie was an exception. She was curves and softness, abundance, and happiness. There was nothing I liked better than seeing her body open before me, all pink skin, and soft curves.

I'm gonna ruin you, Baby Girl.

I pulled a length of the rope free, reaching for Ellie and pulling her into a sitting position. She still faced away from me and I grinned, enjoying her obedience.

"You ever hear of Shibari?"

She shook her head, hair tumbling down her back.

"Japanese bondage. Rope play." I ran the tail of the rope across the skin of her back, enjoying her shiver. "You okay if we play tonight?"

Ellie hesitated and I waited, letting her call the shots.

I liked to dominate, not manipulate. There was a big fucking difference.

"Do I need a safe word?"

"Red means stop. Yellow means slow down, and I'll know if you're good to go if you say so." I reached around, tilting her head back a fraction so she could look at me. "You okay with that?"

"Yes, Runner."

"There are shears in the bedside table, reach over and pull them out for me."

She bent, pulling the drawer free and removing the scissors.

"Will we need them?" she asked softly.

"Never have before, but your safety comes first, Ellie."

She nodded, placing the shears on the table, and settling back into position.

I rewarded her with a kiss to her shoulder, gentle and tender. Teasing her just a little. "Good girl."

I pulled back and Ellie's face dropped, her gaze focusing back on the headboard.

Very good girl.

I looped the length of rope, doubling it, then pulled it over her head, creating a knot between her shoulder blades. Ellie's breathing increased, her body shaking as I shifted, slowly creating knots that ran the length of her front.

"These will be for when I add more around you," I explained, threading the rope, enjoying the slightly drugged look in her eyes as I purposefully grazed the rope across her skin. I finished threading the knots down her body then paused, carefully crafting one that would press against her clit.

"This one is known as the happy knot," I explained, spreading her legs, and positioning the rope. "It'll sit right on your clit."

I swirled a finger through the wet, finding her most sensitive core.

Ellie shifted, her eyes closing as she panted, a little whimper escaping her at my touch.

"Now, gonna press this right here," I placed the knot against her clit. "Feel okay?"

She immediately nodded then groaned, her head falling back her body shuddering slightly.

I grinned, moving back around her body to loop the length in the back. The ritual of tying her, of binding her body took on a new meaning for me as I looped patterns with the rope onto her skin. This was my Ellie, no longer a woman I could live without. As I pulled the rope tight, tying off the final knot, it felt like I was binding her to me.

Fucking hope so.

"Because this is your first time, I'm not going to string you up, suspend you and then fuck you." I told her, stroking her skin, enjoying her panting sighs. "But, Baby Girl, you're definitely gonna come"

I dropped, working my way between her thighs, my tongue tracing the rope's path and finding the treasures it hid.

Ellie was soaking wet, her thighs damp, her body shivering as I laved her, my tongue stroked, my mouth worshipped She tasted like heaven and sin, life and death and everything in between.

She tastes like home.

I groaned, fisting my cock, stroking it as I worked her hot body to completion.

Above me, Ellie shattered, her thighs gripping my head, her body writhing as she rode my mouth.

Fuck, yes.

I slid free a moment before she collapsed, catching her in my arms and laying her gently on her side.

Her legs trembled, her body shaking as I slowly untied the rope, giving her time to breathe.

Ellie blinked up at me as I pulled the rope free from around her neck.

"What about you?"

I grinned, knowing it was pure male satisfaction. "Don't you worry, Baby Girl, we're just getting started."

Chapter Nineteen

Ellie

A girl could definitely get used to this.

I woke with a body that ached in the most delicious of ways, and a man who insisted on making me scream once more before I was allowed up.

The least I could do was make Runner pancakes. Correction, I *thought* about making him pancakes. But by the time I got out of the shower he'd returned from the mess hall with a pile of Yana's pastries, something that smells deliciously decadent, and had an actual pot of coffee brewing.

As in *real* coffee. Nothing like the weak shit we'd been rationing for months. No, this was freshly crushed dark roast in an actual French press.

I take it back. The man can definitely have anal.

"What's that smell?" I asked, sniffing the air.

"Something Yana said would, and I quote, 'blow my brains out with delight.'"

"Well, sign me up." I slid onto a bar stool and reached for one of the steaming bowls. "Oh my God," I moaned around a spoonful of indescribable joy. "What even is this?"

"No idea, but it's damned good," Runner agreed, flashing me a grin. He poured out two mugs of precious coffee then slid one across to me, taking the other and leaning back against the counter to watch me eat.

"You already ate?"

He nodded, taking a sip.

"Oh, I was gonna make you pancakes." I lifted a spoon. "Gotta admit, this is *much* better."

He chuckled. "I appreciate the thought, but you needed sleep. And we need to get going."

"Going?"

He rubbed a thumb against his lips. "Gotta go shopping."

I raised an eyebrow. "As in clothes shopping?"

"You got that list of products you need?"

Ah, the biofuel.

"Up here," I said, tapping the side of my head. "But if you got paper and pen, I can get it down."

He disappeared into his bedroom and came out a moment later holding a notepad and pencil. I listed as I ate, making adjustments to the sizes and quantities, offering alternatives to various parts of the set-up should they be unable to find what I needed.

I savoured the last mouthful of my coffee as I finished the list. "I think that's it."

Runner looked over the list, cocking his head. "You need all this?"

"If you want to produce at scale, yeah." I tapped my pencil on my cheek. "Where did you get the coffee beans from?"

"Brothers in Queensland," Runner answered, still reading through my list. "They live on a plantation up there."

"Do you guys trade?"

126

"Trade?" Runner asked, flicking to the second page. "No, we're all communal. The club looks out for itself."

I leaned forward. "But have you considered setting up a supply chain? When people find out we have fuel or food or whatever else we have, they're gonna want it. If the club becomes a distributor, if they set up a barter or traded system then we could take advantage and get what we want out of it too.People want fuel? They'll trade for it. They don't agree, then we deal with them." My lips quirked. "Or, I should say, you guys will deal with them."

"Fuel for coffee?"

I shrugged, "If your northern brothers have it, then I'm open to cocoa beans as well."

Runner laughed. "Go get your coat. We need to get going." I could see the speculative gleam in his eyes. I smiled, knowing he'd be thinking on my suggestion.

I gestured at the list. "You really know a place where we can get all this?" Even the College struggled and they'd had their own biofuel lab.

"Maybe. Get your coat, Baby Girl."

I hopped down, finding my jacket and following Runner out. The central courtyard was a flurry of activity as a contingent of men plus a few women hurried around.

Ava appeared, her sister, Lottie, trailing.

"I'm coming too," Ava declared, already dressed like a badass, dripping in guns. "I'm not letting you take one of my girls without backup."

Runner sighed, giving me a side glance that asked if I wanted to take care of this.

I shot him a grin. *It's all yours, buddy.*

He narrowed his gaze on me, and I swear I could nearly hear

him say, *you'll pay for that later.*

I couldn't wait.

"No." He brushed passed Ava and I nearly laughed at his foolishness. Ava was not a woman to simply dismiss.

"Uh, not no," Ava corrected, following him. "You find me a bike and I can ride."

"We don't got the fuel to waste."

"Then I'll ride in the truck."

"No room."

"There is if I ride in the back."

Runner stopped, turning to Ava. "You're injured."

"I'm better."

"Not by much," Lottie muttered beside me, glaring at her sister.

Of the two of them, Lottie was the soft one. Riots of curls that flew crazily about her head. She looked like a perpetually mystified art teacher instead of the veterinarian she was.

"You're doing a run. I need stuff, my girls need stuff, your women need stuff." Ava held up a list—all four pages, double sided. "I get these, you get the big stuff, it saves us all in the long run."

"No," Runner repeated. "One, this is an in-out. We're not dawdling. Two, this isn't some shopping spree. We're getting what we need then getting the fuck home. And what we need is already gonna be risky to get without someone trying to shit with us. We don't have guys to spare to assist you."

Ava rolled her eyes. "Self-righteous, much? I don't need your help. I just need a seat and some space in one of the trucks for the stuff on this list."

"It's not all clothes," Lottie offered, wringing her hands. "If Ava gets some of the items, I can shear the sheep that are wandering around your property and turn the raw wool into yarn. We'd be able to make clothing."

Runner crossed his arms over his chest. Hazard chose that moment to arrive, taking in the scene.

"Jesus, what now?" he asked with a sigh.

"They're trying to *little house on the prairie* us," Runner said, glaring at Ava. "Want to go shopping so they can turn this place into a little production line."

I frowned.

"Jesus, sue us for trying to better what we've got." Ava jerked her head at the men. "You think you're gonna be able to wear those clothes forever? What about when they start to shred? You guys may have food, you may be about to have fuel, but God damn it, you're gonna need clothing and a production line at some point to facilitate that." Ava pointed at the Hen House. "You got women who know all this shit. Let me give them what they need so they can teach the other women and maybe even some of your men. Let us be an asset to you, for fuck's sake."

Hazard ran a hand over his face. He looked worse for wear after last night. Not so much hungover as already wearied by the weight of responsibility on his shoulders.

"What's your objection, Runner?" he finally asked.

"We didn't bring them here to be slaves," Runner barked. "Don't want anyone working on production lines."

Hazard looked to his friend and I saw the flash of understanding cross his face. "Ava, the women. Do they want to contribute or is this something they're doing because they feel they have to?"

"We want to," Lottie answered. "We're all in this together. The least we could do is make things less shitty."

Hazard nodded. "Runner, find another truck and get two of the prospects to go along." He held out a hand, taking Ava's list and perusing it. "Scope out the other women on the property. See if they need anything." He pulled a pen from his pocket, making a note. He handed it back to Ava and she looked down, reading his addition. Her head shot up in surprise.

"We got kids here," he muttered. A man called for the President, and Hazard sighed. "Duty calls." He turned on his heel and headed for the gathered group of men nearby.

"I've never seen a guy less happy to be in charge," Lottie remarked as we watched him walk away.

Ava shrugged. "Sometimes those most reluctant make the best leaders." She tucked the list into her back pocket. "So, we good?"

Runner sighed, "We're good. Let's find you a working truck."

Chapter Twenty

Ellie

Runner cruised to a stop, parking his ride. This was our first stop, a home improvement warehouse in the middle of an industrial park. The place looked pretty stripped, but the size of it meant that there was likely to be a few items that people hadn't thought to pillage.

"Off Ellie," he directed, looking around. "We got an hour."

The trucks we'd brought rolled to a stop, Ava immediately jumping down and coming to me. "You ready?"

I nodded. "Let's do this."

Runner caught my hand, pulling me back. "Be safe," he instructed, pressing a kiss to my hair. "Stay with Ava, stay with the guys, get what you need then straight back here."

I nodded.

He hesitated for a moment then nodded. "Okay, go."

As much as I wanted to stay with him, I'd be better doing the small stuff—like collecting tubes, rope, and the like.

Ava handed me a handgun and I tucked it in my waistband, appreciating its comforting weight.

"Here." One of the club members handed me an empty duffle

bag. "Fill it with what you need, then fill it with anything else that will fit."

"Anything?"

"You never know when something'll come in handy."

True.

We walked inside as the rest of the men split between two groups, one concentrating on raiding the big stuff and getting that loaded, the other setting up a security perimeter.

"Stay close," Ava muttered as we entered the building. "God knows if there's any packrats holed up here."

We stopped in the big entry, bikers heading down either side of the giant warehouse, checking the aisles for dangers.

"Come on," Ava murmured. "Let's go get your shit."

We headed towards plumbing, Ava on watch for threats, me scanning the aisles for the items I needed, dodging the mess on the floor. Our footsteps left prints in the dirt as we moved. I noted that the warehouse showed signs of returning to nature; leaves, sticks, cobwebs, and insects decorated the floors and shelving. The occasional bird flapped to life, startled by the humans prowling through their nesting grounds.

"Here," I whispered, halting Ava's movements.

The majority of the warehouse had been picked over. Things that had some form of value or had some easy use had been pilfered long ago. But the aisles that contained things like plumbing or building materials were mostly untouched. For one, they were specialised items, not easy to use if you weren't familiar with them. For another, they were bulky, not easy to transport when you had to walk everywhere. Apart from wood, which for the most part had been taken. It'd been a cold winter and little was left apart from the largest logs and poles.

I dropped the duffle bag, reaching for the shelving, putting my feet to the bottom shelf.

"What are you doing?"

"We need to get the boxes at the top."

Ava looked up then swore. "Really?"

I nodded.

She blew out a breath. "You can't climb that."

"Why not?"

Ava un-looped the rifle strap from around her body, holding it out for me to take. "No offence, but you have zero upper body strength. Meanwhile I can bench press double my body weight." She shot me a grin. "I got this."

"What about your side?"

She ignored me, reaching up to the shelf just above her head. Without even a grunt, she pulled herself up, scrambling up the side of the shelving to the dusty boxes.

"What are you after?" Ava called, looking at all the boxes.

"Throw it all down, I'm not sure what I'll need."

The first box hit the ground with a dull thud, not too loud but still enough to startle. I heard footsteps start running our way and I raised the rifle bracing myself.

"Put it down," Ava called. "It's just some of your boyfriend's buddies."

Ice skidded to a halt, looking from me at the foot of the shelving, and up to see Ava heaving another box over the side.

"Jesus Christ," Ice barked. "Warning next time."

"Just open the damn boxes," I replied, crouching to rip open the cardboard.

The next several minutes were spent sorting.

"Oh baby," Ava called from the end of one shelving unit. "You'll never believe what I found up here!"

I looked up to see her lifting a small box from a larger one holding it up in triumph.

I squinted trying to read the label. "What is it?"

She threw the box down, Ice catching it easily. He handed it over to me and I grinned. "Seeds."

"There's a whole goddamned box up here. Miracle that they're completely sealed. The rats haven't gotten to them."

"Must have been misplaced at some stage," Ice muttered, leaning closer to read the side of the box. "Lucky for us."

I hugged the starter kit close. Ava grunted, shoving the giant box and sending it tumbling to the ground. It landed with a loud thud, and Ice immediately started picking over it, checking the damage.

"We're good."

"Kate will be happy." Ava climbed down, jumping the last few feet to land beside us. "Call your boys. We should probably check the other boxes."

"No time," Ice replied, packing up the starter packs and lifting the big box. "We've gotta head out."

I grabbed my stuffed duffle bags, then gestured at the leftover boxes. "We should store these somewhere. We might need replacement items."

Ava shook her head. "We either take what we need now or we assume it's not going to be here when we get back."

I chewed my lip. "Far out."

"We need to go," Ice repeated, jostling the box. "Get your shit."

I handed a bag to Ava then paused, catching a glimpse of something through the shelves.

"Wait, I have a solution."

I ran around the aisle, laughing as I tugged the manual forklift free. "Perfect."

I wheeled it around, Ava chuckling as soon as she caught sight of it. "Good idea, Ellie."

We loaded the boxes, Ice carrying the duffle bags, and Ava leading as we moved out.

Outside, the men were loading the trucks, the final big containers being rolled onto the back.

I caught sight of Runner, sweaty and flushed as he lifted a water tank onto the back of one of the utes.

"Man is fit," Ava muttered beside me, also watching.

"Hands off," I laughed, pushing the cart forward. "He's mine."

"Who said I was looking at Runner?"

"Who were you—"

A gun shot cracked through the air.

Ava shoved me to the ground, throwing herself on top of me.

I looked up, my heart freezing when I saw the blood.

Chapter Twenty-One

Runner

I'm gonna rip the motherfucker apart.

I crouched beside the truck, gun in hand, waiting for the bullets to stop raining down on us. In the middle of the open carpark, Ava, Ice and Ellie lay flat, protected only by three pitifully flimsy boxes.

"Ice is hit!"

"Fuck."

"Found him," Ghost grunted beside me. "Top of the warehouse, left side."

I looked up, spotting the idiot with a gun.

"You got a shot?" I asked.

"Not with a pistol."

The sniper rifle was in the back of the truck. Which gave us two options; we either wait for the fucker on the roof to finish his shooting spree or distract him long enough to allow time for either Ghost or Hazard to get to the rifle.

"Where's Hazard?"

"Pegged down by the fence."

Shit.

I calculated the risk, my brain processing a million miles a minute.

"Gonna draw his fire. You know what to do."

Ghost nodded once.

"Keep my girl safe," I ordered. I took a breath, throwing one last glance at Ellie, who was lying flat on the ground, her arms folded across her head, her cheek pressed to the gravel. Bracing, I sprinted, heading towards the corner of the warehouse where the guy had holed up.

A bullet ricocheted on my left, immediately followed by rapid fire.

Bring it on, motherfucker.

I'd gotten my name not because I ran drugs or guns, though I'd done that before our club had decided to go legit. No, I'd gotten the name because I was the fastest fucker in the club. I'd run a target down in my first week, earning me the moniker.

Bullets pelted the ground around me as I sprinted, head down, arms pumping.

Ellie.

If I died it would be for her. One of my brothers would take my place, keeping her warm, occupying her bed. It wouldn't do to have her mourning me forever. Not when life was short, danger everywhere, and our time together so brief.

But God, the thought wrecked me. It hurt so fucking bad that I couldn't imagine any outcome other than the one where I was balls deep in her tonight. Her cunt clenching around me, her body arching as I filled her with my seed.

I refuse to let this fucker kill us.

A bullet hit my shoulder, tearing at the flesh. I stumbled, but righted quickly, sprinting the last few feet to plaster myself against the building. The slight overhang protecting me from his fire.

I pulled my gun free, rounding the corner of the building, searching for stairs to take me to the roof.

If Ghost failed, I needed to be plan B.

A shot rang out, one single crack splitting through the uneven shooting. Silence followed.

Make sure he's dead.

I made for the stairs, climbing the rusted metal, gun raised. I paused at the top, crouching, watching for movement.

A body slumped against the roof wall, unmoving but for the blood pooling from the hole in his head.

There was a shanty up here, a makeshift tent city, filled with weapons and a shit ton of explosives. I made my way through the area, clearing it, making sure this guy was the only threat.

There're enough explosives here to blow up half the country.

Satisfied we were alone and nothing was rigged to explode if we made a wrong move, I made my way back to the piece of shit slumped against the wall. His brains were blown out, the skin, bone, and tissue splattered over his weapons cache.

I looked over the side signalling that I needed some help. No way were we leaving this here, it was a God damned gold mine.

I scoped the parking lot, finding Ellie by the truck. From this distance I couldn't make out if she was hurt, but she glanced my way, fully turning to shoot me a thumbs up. I blew out a breath, my heart settling back into my chest.

Hazard made it up first, his gaze immediately dropping to my shoulder, his mouth tightening.

"Get to the fucking truck. You're heading home."

I shook my head. "It's just a graze."

"Yeah, and I'm a fucking mother of dragons," Hazard bit back. "Get to the truck. The women are loading Ice. He needs medical attention. I want you there as well."

I glanced back at the piles of explosives. "What about—"

"We'll handle it, Runner. Just get in the fucking truck." Hazard clapped a hand on my good shoulder. "You did good. But I can't risk losing another man today."

My heart seized. "Who?"

His eyes met mine, stricken, his face awash with grief. "Silver. Stray bullet caught a fucking artery. We couldn't stop the bleeding."

I sucked in a breath. Silver was old, in his late sixties. Stubborn as a fucking ox. A loss to the club.

"He's free to ride now," I said, knowing it was a hollow sympathy.

"His body's being loaded," Hazard shot me a look. "Just go, Runner."

I nodded, heading out as grim-faced brothers began the task of carefully packing up the explosives and ammunition.

I found Ellie in the backseat of the truck, Ava loading the last package in the back as one of the prospects started the engine.

"Baby Girl," I called and she shot me a look over her shoulder, blood dotting her face.

I immediately crossed to her, almost pulling her out, cupping her cheek and forcing her to look at me.

"It's not mine," she said, pulling back. "I'm okay."

"I'll be the judge of—"

"Get in the fucking truck," Ava barked. "We need to get Ice to Blair."

I helped Ellie back in, then rounded the truck, getting in on the other side.

Ice slumped in the middle seat, Ellie pressing hands against his leg. He was pale, sweaty, shaking.

"You right man?" I asked as Ava hopped in the front seat, the truck pulling away a moment later.

"I'll be fine." He tried to smile but it looked more like a gritting of teeth. "Think the doc will give me the good drugs?"

"Depends if you're a good boy," I replied, leaning over, and removing Ellie's hand for a moment to examine the wound. Flesh, lots of blood, likely a little bit of bone but no major arteries.

Thank God.

The ride back was a shit fight. Ice trying not to pass out as the truck bumped along the road, the drive long and his pain level high.

"Not much longer," I murmured sometime later, keeping the pressure against his leg. We'd shifted him, his back to Ellie's front, his leg raised so I could apply pressure to the wound.

Blood covered the back seat of the SUV, despite our best efforts.

The truck jarred again, and Ice bit out a curse, slumping into Ellie. She rubbed his arms, reassuring him.

"Runner, if… if I don't…." Ice cleared his throat. "Tell Kate I love her."

"Shut up you baby," I ordered. "You can tell her your fucking self."

We pulled into the compound, horn beeping, heading straight for the infirmary.

Blair and Butcher appeared in the doorway, Blair glaring, Butcher's arms crossed as they watched us approach.

The prospect pulled to a stop, but Ava was already out, yelling for help.

The following moments were fraught as we transported Ice from the truck to the infirmary, Butcher and Blair barking orders, questioning the patient, Ava and Ellie explaining what happened.

I lifted Ice onto the waiting bed, then stepped back.

"Get Aella," Blair ordered Ellie. "We need extra hands."

Ellie pivoted, taking off.

"Aella?" I asked Ava who looked exhausted.

"She's our nurse. Helps Blair with the big stuff." She rubbed a hand over her face. "Come on, let's get this stuff unloaded."

My shoulder protested but there was nothing I could do at the moment. The bleeding had slowed, my shirt soaking up most of the blood.

At least it's black, maybe I can repair it.

Clothing was in short supply around here, and this was a decent shirt.

Ellie returned, the other woman in tow. They disappeared inside as we began to unload some of the items that were specifically for the infirmary.

We'd rolled out a large water container, leaning it against the wall of the building when Ellie reappeared, her hands now clean of blood. She made a beeline for me, coming to wrap her arm around me and lay her head on my shoulder.

I hissed in pain.

She pulled back, hands immediately coming to my shoulder, searching for the wound, blood coating her cheek. "You're hurt!"

I bit out a laugh, "Nah, just clipped a little. It's nothing to worry about."

She pushed up my shirt, peeling it from my body.

Ellie sucked in a breath as she discarded the material, her face grimacing.

"That bad huh?"

"Looks like minced meat."

I glanced down, noting the torn skin and bruising. It wouldn't kill me but it wasn't pleasant. Would definitely need stitches.

"Looks worse than it feels," I lied.

"Liar," she immediately replied, pulling me behind her. "Let's go."

"They're with Ice," I protested. "I can wait."

"Yeah, you can wait inside where I can clean it out while they finish with Ice and then you can get stitched up."

She sounded angry. And worried. God, I hated to worry her.

I pulled her to a stop, turning her until I could look into her exhausted, anxious eyes.

"Baby Girl, I'm okay." I reassured, brushing a hand across her face. "It's just a scratch. It'll heal."

Her chin wobbled but she stiffened it, biting out, "You ran right at him. You nearly died."

"But I didn't."

"I'm so angry with you."

My eyebrows raised in question but she shook her head. "Come with me."

Chapter Twenty-Two

Runner

They'd knocked Ice out, giving him something Butcher had concocted a few years back. It knocked you out and left you numb for a few hours before you woke up with a hangover and a hard-on.

Not fun but damned effective in a shitty situation.

Ellie led me to the main room, pushing me onto a stool beside a long bench. I watched her, ignoring the surgery going on mere feet from us. Concentrating on the sound of the water as she switched it on, the way her hands glided together as she soaped them up, the look of concentration and concern as she scrubbed her finger nails.

Satisfied, she used her elbow to switch the tap off, then reached for gloves from a box hanging above the sink. The movement lifted her shirt just a fraction, enough that I could see the smooth, soft skin of her belly.

I'd been in crisis mode earlier. Needing to prioritise the safety of her, of Ice, of Ava. Focused on getting the explosives sorted so no prick with a pistol could hurt my woman.

But now? The adrenaline was starting to crash, but instead

of exhaustion, which I knew would come, I felt horny. I wanted to claim Ellie. To mark her. To push her onto a bed and pin her down as I made her come again and again until I worked out the fear and anger that bubbled just under my skin.

She could have been killed.

She'd filled a small container with warm water and antiseptic, and now stood over me, examining the wound. It put her tits right at eye level, giving me a great view even as pain flared as she gently prodded the area.

"I'll clean this up, there's some dirt in here. But I'll leave it to the others to stitch. I'd try but I'd likely leave you with a giant arse scar."

Call me a sadist, but I liked the idea that she'd leave a mark on my skin. A tangible, visible marker that she was mine and I was hers.

She dipped a cotton bud in the water then brought it to my shoulder, gently brushing at the wound. I bit back a curse, pain blossoming out from the wound site.

"Does it hurt?" she asked softly, her hands steady but her eyes bright with tears.

"Nah," I lied. "More like a bee sting."

Her lips trembled a little as if she knew I was lying. But she didn't press, instead turning back to the site and discarding one used cotton bud for a new one. Ellie cleaned it slowly, reverently, and with a thoroughness I had to admire.

"Why were you upset earlier?" Ellie asked quietly, her concentration focussed on the wound. "When Ava suggested we start making clothes."

Her eyes flicked up, catching my look then darting back to my shoulder. "Don't you like clothes?"

I grimaced, breathing out from between clenched teeth as

144

she scrubbed a particularly deep tear. "It's not that. I agree that we need to reconsider how we do shit. Clothes ain't gonna just make themselves."

I hesitated as she turned, dropping the dirty cotton bud in a container then selecting another one, gently wetting it in the antiseptic solution.

"But?" she prompted softly.

"But my mum worked in a factory. From the day she was old enough to the day she died. Sitting at the same goddamned workstation. Less than minimum wage, treated no better than a dog. Her hands were arthritic by the time she was forty. But still she went because she didn't have any other goddamned fucking options."

I gritted my teeth, closing my eyes and focussing on the sting from Ellie's ministrations, rather than the ache of regret that forever burned in my chest.

"Two days after I convinced her to retire, to move in with me she had a stroke and died."

Ellie flinched. "Shit, Runner. I'm so sorry."

I blew out a breath. "Thanks."

She touched a cotton bud to my shoulder, hesitating for a moment. "So, she's why you don't want us doing the work?"

I shook my head. "Nah. We need to do it, I know that. But the suggestion brought up bad memories."

She nodded. "I'm sorry."

Ellie pressed a kiss to my cheek, then turned to the sink, emptying the leftover water. Used cotton buds overflowed from a small container, red with my blood.

The door to the infirmary burst open, and I surged up, pegging Ellie to the sink, covering her with my body.

"Where is he?" Kate demanded, standing in the entry. She

caught sight of Ice on the bed and flew into the room.

"Stop!' Blair ordered.

Kate halted, tears glistening. I relaxed my stance, letting Ellie up from the sink.

"Does he need blood?" she asked, her gaze falling to the trail on the floor.

"He will," Butcher replied, threading a stitch through Ice's skin.

"He's A negative. Can only have O positive or A negative blood." She held out a trembling arm. "I'm A negative."

All eyes went to her, the operation on the table stilling.

"You're related?" Aella asked.

Kate's lip wobbled but she nodded once. "Yeah. Gus was his father too. Another discarded offspring of a man who was obsessed with spreading his seed everywhere but in his wife."

"Did you know?" Ellie asked me softly.

"Fuck no. Thought they were sweet on each other."

Ellie shuddered. "Glad this isn't a Lannister sibling situation."

I raised an eyebrow, *"Game of Thrones?"*

"Loved it but for the ending." She made face. "Guess we won't be getting the written ending we deserve either."

"Aella, can you get Kate sorted?" Blair asked, pulling a thread as she stitched Ice. "Butcher and I can handle this."

I watched for a moment as Aella settled Kate onto a chair, bustling to get the blood transfusion set up.

When she finished with Kate, Aella came to me, stepping close to examine the wound.

"Needs stitches." She washed, then got what she needed, threading the hooked needle, and disinfecting the wound. "I'll give you an antibiotic shot after. You want pain relief?"

I shook my head.

Aella rolled her eyes but immediately set to threading, murmuring, "Okay, tough guy. Stay still, this might hurt."

I ignored the pain, concentrating instead on Ellie. She stood behind Aella, holding a torch over the wound site, biting her lip every time the needle went through my skin, and wincing every time Aella pulled the thread tight.

"You're done." Aella slapped a bandage on the site. "Keep it clean and dry. Add some antiseptic every twenty-four hours. If you have any issues, come back." She discarded her gloves and equipment, brushing a hand across her forehead to remove the long strands of dark hair. "Now get out of here, go rest. You can deal with the other shit later."

She turned, pausing. "And if you see Ava, send her our way. God knows the woman has probably stressed her stitches. She needs to be resting, not running around the place as if she's GI Joe."

I nodded, letting Ellie wrap an arm around me and guide me out of the room.

I didn't need the assistance, but she felt damned good snuggled against me.

Chapter Twenty-Three

Runner

I waited 'til we reached our room and Ellie had shut the door before I crowded her, pressing her against the door as I gripped the back of her head with one hand, my fingers tugging at her strands, tipping her face to give me access to her neck.

I couldn't fight the desire that had been running rampant in me since the shooting had begun. I pressed a long kiss to her neck then gave in, sucking, teeth grazing, knowing I was giving her a mark and revelling in that knowledge.

If I could, I'd have tattooed my name on her, branding this woman as mine. Satisfaction, desire, need, they warred in me, fighting for dominance as she squirmed under me.

"Runner, stop. Just, stop."

I didn't. I kept kissing her neck, glorying in her taste.

"Red!"

I pulled back instantly, dropping my arms, and taking a step back.

"Fuck, Ellie. You okay, baby?" Ellie held up a hand, glaring at me.

"Babe?"

"I've held it in until we were alone but—" She sucked in a deep breath, her eyes flashing angrily as her hands came to her hips. "What. Do you think. You're *fucking* doing?" she gritted out.

I frowned. "Kissing you."

"You're a fucking idiot!" she roared, coming at me. "You could have died!" She beat her hands on my chest and I let her, enjoying the sting of her aggression, of her passion.

"You can't leave me here, Runner! Not now. Not because some jerk with a gun decides to take pot shots. You hear me?" She looked up, her eyes meeting mine. For a moment they radiated anger, all her fear channelled at me as glorious rage. Then she crumbled, tears falling down her beautiful cheeks, her body collapsing into mine.

"Hey." I caught her as she fell, gently easing us both to the floor. "I'm okay, Baby Girl."

She sobbed into me, her arms reaching up to twine around my neck. "You got shot."

"But I'm here. It's a scratch."

"You got stitches!"

"And I'll get stitches again, no doubt." I pulled her into my lap, cradling her close. "I want to tell you I'll always be fine, Ellie. I want to tell you we'll be together forever, and I'll never put myself into a position where I'm in danger. But I can't."

She jerked, pulling away, but I didn't let her get far.

I brushed tears from her cheek with the knuckles of one hand. "I'm sorry, Baby Girl. I can't give you those platitudes, not in the after. Not now when you've got psychos shooting from roof tops, and danger around every corner."

I blew out a breath. "But while we're together, I can promise you this. It's just you and me. I'm going to make you mine,

Ellie. In our club that means property. You'll be my old lady. You'll wear my name on your back, and you'll be untouchable. If I die, you get to choose what comes next, but either way my brothers will take care of you. They'll throw down for you, love you, protect you like I would."

Her lip wobbled but she bit it, tears shimmering but no longer falling.

"I love you, Ellie. Baby Girl, I can't imagine a life without you." I leaned forward, pressing my forehead to hers. "Will you give me this, Ellie? Will you agree to being my old lady?"

She nodded but I need the words.

"Say it."

"I'm yours, Runner. Today, tomorrow, forever. As long as you'll have me."

I shifted us, gently laying her onto the floor. I pulled her jeans from her body, discarding them and then pulled my own down, only far enough to free my cock.

I wedged a hand between us, my fingers finding her wet little clit. I played with her, pressing as she panted beneath me, hot little whimpers escaping her body.

"You want this, Baby Girl? You want me in your greedy little cunt?"

She moaned, and I grinned. Fierce possession still rode me hard, but I needed her to be as desperate as I felt. Needed her aching and begging for my cock as I fed it to her.

Her scent perfumed the air, her slick arousal coating my hands and her thighs as I continued to stroke her, play with her, worshipping my woman.

I bit the side of her neck, immediately kissing away the sting. Her hands raked my back, her lips moving over my chest, my good shoulder, my neck.

CHAPTER TWENTY-THREE

"Lips," she demanded. "Need to taste you. Please, Runner."

I allowed that, granting her wish, knowing it would feed her need.

"Close," she panted against my lips. "So close."

I pressed her, capturing her protest with my mouth, using her gasp to slip my tongue past her lips as I withdrew my hand. I swiftly replaced my hand with my cock, rubbing her, coating my shaft with her arousal.

"You ready, Baby Girl? You want this?" I asked, teasing her, drawing out the anticipation.

"Yes," she breathed, her eyes wide, feverish. "Please."

"Please what?"

"Please, Runner. Please…."

I grinned, knowing it was feral, knowing it was a grin filled with satisfaction and desire and my filthy fucking fantasies.

"Gonna fuck you right here, Ellie girl. Gonna fuck you raw today. Fill you with my cum. Then I'm gonna fuck you with my fingers until you come again. Then we're going in the bedroom and I'm gonna start all the fuck over again."

And then I thrust, hard and fast. She was tight, so fucking tight. I had to work her, stretch her, both of us beginning to shatter as she adjusted, her hot little cunt accommodating me.

"You like this, don't you, Baby Girl? You like me owning this hot little pussy, don't you?"

She groaned, head tipping back, hips tilting up, granting me more access as I thrust into her, fucking her with a steady, hard, purposeful rhythm.

I reached up, hand cupping her throat, pressing just enough to get her attention, to make her open her gorgeous eyes and look at me.

"Say it."

"Yes, Runner." The words were no sooner out of her mouth than my control snapped. I fucked her into the floorboards, thrusting again and again as she cried out, urging me to go faster, harder, her body welcoming me. When she finally shattered, her entire being vibrating with her orgasm. Clutching at my cock, her pussy milked me. But it wasn't enough. I gripped her head, bringing her mouth to my chest.

"Bite me," I ordered, my thrusts now brutal. "Fucking mark me, Ellie. Do it!"

Her teeth gripped my skin and the sharp pain, brutal and desperate, tipped me over. I broke, my cock pumping into her again and again, my cum painting her insides.

"Fuck yes," I grunted, "fuck Baby Girl. Fuck."

We collapsed, Ellie languid and panting under me. The blood still thundered through my veins; my need barely dented.

I rolled off her, then sat up, hand gliding down her body as I leaned over her, my face close to hers.

"Brace, Baby Girl. I'm not even close to fucking done."

I captured her lips, our tongues tangling as I fucked her with my fingers, finding her G-spot and pressing. Showing absolutely no mercy. She bucked under me, hands desperately clawing at my arm, my back; her legs shifting restlessly as I forced her to come again for me, relishing the knowledge that some of the wet on my finger was my cum. Fucking her with it, some distant, primitive part of my brain roaring approval.

Ellie broke, her mouth tearing from mine, her body arching, rippling as she came, a scream breaking free.

"Own it," I ordered. "Take it, Ellie. Fucking own your pleasure."

She did, riding my hand, clenching until finally, after a long moment she dropped, her body sated.

She panted, trying to catch her breath and I gave her that pause. It took her a minute but finally, she looked at me, blinking as if this were the first time she'd seen me.

"Runner?"

"Yeah, Baby Girl?"

"Wow."

I chuckled; her smile was infectious, beautiful, stunning. I felt lighter than I had in days. "Fucking oath, Baby Girl. Fucking oath."

Chapter Twenty-Four

Ellie

The thing about the after was that there was little downtime. Where before it may have been permissible to spend a full day in bed with Runner, in the after there were people who relied on us—who relied on me—to produce. To keep things running.

We arrived at the warehouse early but already there were men and women walking around, surveying the big shed.

"Your rodeo, Baby Girl," Runner told me. "Let the people know what you need."

The first step to setting up my lab was making it clean and weatherproof. The warehouse had once been used for storage, as evidenced by the large shelving units stacked to one side.

There were a few minor leaks in the roof, likely from storms rather than significant structural issues. While they hadn't been used in close to twenty years, the bikers had kept the sheds in decent condition.

While the men dealt with the external issues, the women and a few prospects got to work cleaning the interior and setting up work stations. Birds needed to be removed, leaves and dust cleared out. The purity of the fuel depended upon a sterile work environment, if dirt got into the mix, it could damage engines.

In a surprisingly short amount of time, the lab began to come together.

We broke for lunch, Yana arriving with a car full of sandwiches and snacks. I moved to help her unpack, but Beast intercepted, nudging me aside and lifting a full crate from the trunk.

"He's useful to have around," Yana remarked, watching him carry the heavy load to a makeshift table we'd set up in the sun.

"And not bad to look at," I added, giving her a hip bump.

He wasn't pretty like Pope, or handsome like Runner. But there was an earthy, ruggedness to him. He radiated power, drawing the eye with both his size and beautifully marked skin.

Yana rolled her eyes. "A man like that isn't going to be interested in a woman like me."

I raised an eyebrow, giving her a look.

"He's only interested in food. I'm a chef. That's the extent of it."

I hesitated, wondering if I should intervene. I'd seen how he looked at her, as if he were starving and she a full feast.

Runner came up, looping his arm around me, pulling me against him.

"Let them sort it out," he murmured in my ear, nuzzling my hair.

I laughed, looking up at him. "How did you know?"

He shrugged, giving me a filthy grin. "Wanna show you something."

I felt his erection press against the curve of my butt.

"I think I've already seen your 'something.'"

He chuckled, twisting us until his arm hooked around my

shoulders and I was pressed into his side. He walked us away from the gathering, telling one of the prospects to save us some food.

Catcalls and friendly ribbing followed us. He raised a hand, flicking them the bird but we continued, walking past my lab and into the next warehouse.

"Need your opinion." He gestured with his free hand to the space. "A brother wants to set this up as a greenhouse. Thoughts?"

Which brother?

"It'd work," I said, imagining how we could do it. "We'd need a lot of equipment though. And either energy to run halogens or we'd have to modify the roof to allow for sunlight."

"You think Kate would be open to helping with it?"

I nodded. "Makes sense to get it up and running. But this is a conversation you should have with her."

"But then how would I get you alone?" Runner crowded me, easing us back until my back pressed against a wall. "Need to taste you, Baby Girl."

I huffed out a laugh, my body immediately responding. "You're insatiable"

"Only because you taste so good."

He dropped, pulling down my jeans and underwear, his mouth immediately finding me.

"So wet, Baby Girl."

I sighed as he teased me with tongue and lips, his fingers joining to drive me higher. As I teetered on the edge of climax, we were interrupted by a cough.

Runner pulled back, gun raised, glaring in the direction of the cough.

"Wrath," he greeted.

"Runner." The man stepped out of the shadows, rubbing a hand through his hair. He looked exhausted, dark circles ringed his eyes, his face gaunt.

I reached down, tugging up my jeans and covering myself, my cheeks hot with embarrassment.

"What're you doing in here?" Runner asked, getting to his feet, and holstering his gun.

"Trying to catch a few winks, thought this would be as good a place as any to bed down"

I looked beyond him, squinting into the dark to see a pallet on the floor, no more than a thin sleeping bag and a backpack hidden between the metal shelving units.

"You're bringing news from the Plantation?" Runner asked. Wrath nodded.

"Good news?"

"Your President'll be calling Church tonight. I'll update you then."

Your President?

Runner nodded. "Wrath, this is Ellie, my old lady."

Wrath took me in with dark eyes and a grim face. I wasn't sure what he saw as he looked at me, but his eyes held a glimmer of approval.

"Nice to meet you, Ellie." He tucked hands into his jean pockets, leaning against a shelving unit. "You're one of the girls Kate brought."

It wasn't a question but I still answered with a nod.

He considered me but asked nothing further.

"How did you know about us being here?" I asked.

"Met Whip on the road. Got the update."

Whip, the club's Secretary, had been the biker dispatched the night Gus had been overthrown. Chief had tasked him with delivering the message of the changeover to the other chapters.

Wrath's lips twisted down. "Don't know if your boy will make it back. The fuel stops are running on fumes. Barely managed to baby my ride here last night."

I felt Runner tense beside me, his head bowing for a moment. A tension-filled silence followed.

"She's well, if you wanted to know. Kate, I mean." I finally said, needing to break the silence. "She's sorting seeds up at the Hen House today. We found a box."

Wrath raised an eyebrow. "Hen House?"

"Where the women are staying," I clarified.

Wrath didn't react. I wasn't sure what to make of this man with his black as sin eyes.

"You heard about Ice yet?" Runner asked.

He shook his head. "Got in early this morning, came straight here."

Runner filled him in on the events since Gus' overthrow. His face remained impassive, simply absorbing the news.

Wrath looked around at the warehouse. "This one still available?"

"We were thinking about converting it to a greenhouse but you decide you wanna settle here then it's yours, brother. Always has been."

Wrath considered the large space. "We'll see." He looked back at Runner. "Hazard?"

"Up at the Club House."

He nodded. "Guess I better pay my respects."

"Come grab some food first. The brother's will be happy to see you."

We returned to the assembled workers, sharing food with Wrath before he took off, headed out to find Hazard.

The rest of the afternoon was spent setting up the lab inside. I directed where items needed to go, set up tables, and showed them how to connect equipment to build the different parts of the biofuel set-up.

On the roof, Pope, Beast and Ghost installed solar panels, pilfered from houses and businesses that no longer needed them.

As the sun began to set, Runner pulled me close. Most of the workforce had left, just a few prospects remained, hanging around cleaning up.

"What do you think?" he asked, settling his chin on my shoulder.

The lab was now airtight, the lights and other electrical outlets would be wired tomorrow but the main equipment was set up, ready for use.

"It'll do nicely," I said, leaning back against him. "I just hope it works."

"It will," Runner said, pressing a kiss to my neck. "You got this, Baby Girl."

I hope so.

Chapter Twenty-Five

Runner

Church was in session.

Hazard had weighed his conversation with Wrath and called the brother's together to hear what the club's National President had decreed.

Texas, our tail-gunner, and the stand-in Secretary for Whip, called us to order.

"Alright, settle the fuck down," he called, slapping hands on the table. Previously, Gus would've called us to order, banging that fucking gavel. But Hazard's first decision had been to burn the fucking thing, explaining that this was an opportunity to start afresh.

"First agenda item is fines and finances." He nodded at me.

I ran through the outstanding workloads, assigning the shitty work like septic tank disposal or stall mucking as fines. Only a few grumbled. The rest of the roster was allocated and settled quickly.

Texas gestured at Wrath. "And now a word from our magnanimous messenger boy."

There were sniggers around the table but the levity was lost within moments.

"Shield's retreated to the Plantation. They're recalling the local chapters."

Silence dominated the room.

Shield, the club's National President, had been transferring between chapters for the last few months. Checking on the clubs, keeping everyone moving. Last update had come before an end of season cold snap had slowed the other brothers. At that time, word had been that Shield was planning to make his way down to us, visiting with each chapter in-between.

"What changed?" Chief asked. I glanced at Hazard, finding his face blank as he watched the gathered men process the news.

"Fuel." Wrath ran a hand through his hair. "And the army. And zealots, cannibals, and preppers. Not to mention the cartel, groups of roving grifters, bastards and the odd lunatic who just wants to watch the world burn."

Wrath shook his head. "Our safe houses are still good, or at least they were last I checked. But the fuel supplies are low. Without a steady resupply we're all gonna be fucked."

Communications were down, had been since the country went dark. We'd been exploring options like telegraph or even fucking carrier pigeon, but no one had been able to figure out how to make that work yet. As an interim, brothers like Wrath, nomads with no home club, travelled up and down the coast, delivering messages and sharing news.

If the fuel dried up then we'd be fucked.

"Why'd Shield pull them back to the Plantation?"

The Plantation was a sprawling, luxurious estate up in Lake Proserpine. Once owned by the cartel, the brothers had taken it over a decade back. I wasn't sure what had happened, but once it'd exchanged hands, Shield had razed it, rebuilding it into a fucking fortress.

"Shield's consolidating. The chapters are facing extinction if we don't protect our people. He wants us to enact Plan B."

Wrath pulled a long cylinder from his bag. He unscrewed the top, removing rolled sheets of paper from a protected plastic bag. He spread them across the table, placing stones on each corner to keep them in place. He nodded at Ghost near the door.

"Lights, brother."

Ghost turned them off, then hit the black light, revealing a glowing map.

The map and it's accompanied explanation outlined Shield's plan. All chapters were to consolidate in three major points. Up at the Plantation, at the Cunnamulla chapter's bunker, or here in the compound. Here, Hazard would remain President—at least for the moment.

But there were stipulations, including a fight night where the president would be the last one standing, if Hazard's leadership was disputed. Goddamned unlucky son of a bitch.

"Shield's sending men to all the chapters. They have a choice, join you or leave."

"When do you go back?" Chief asked.

Wrath glanced at Hazard who nodded, his face still blank.

"I don't. Shield's directed that all nomads need a home base until otherwise ordered." Wrath's lips twisted. It wasn't a smile, but it wasn't a grimace either. "I'm here for the long term, kids."

Around the table, the brothers began to stir. Ghost swapped the lights back.

"Continue," Hazard ordered, his voice immediately silencing the gathering.

"Shield's sent Rizzo to head up Cunnamulla. "

"Rizzo's a loss for Shield," Chief remarked. The man had been Shield's Vice President since he'd taken carriage.

"Too much unrest around Cunnamulla. He needed a strong leader to bring them together." Wrath sighed. "Besides, Shield has bigger problems." Wrath rubbed a hand across his face. "My orders were to let the relevant chapters know and then notify you guys. The chapters were meant to arrive next week, giving you guys enough time to prepare, and them enough time to pack their shit and get here." His jaw clenched. "Only Canberra and Jindabyne are coming. The rest were already gone."

"Gone?" Pope asked.

Wrath glanced at Hazard who nodded, granting permission.

Wrath pulled out two notes from his pocket. "Two said they were headed to the Plantation. Winter and drought had hit them hard and their supplies were low. I didn't see them on the road but that doesn't mean anything these days." He swallowed. "Wollongong was a slaughter house. Two brothers remained; both had been out hunting when the club had been hit. There wasn't a man left alive. The kids and women were taken. Same thing in Nowra, only no survivors and all the women and children vanished."

The brothers snapped. Standing, punching walls, shouting.

Only Ghost, Hazard, Wrath, and I remained seated.

Wrath and Hazard likely because they'd already processed the news. While Ghost and I, we'd seen something like this before.

My eyes met his over the table. He jerked his head up, acknowledging my unspoken question.

"Quiet!" Hazard roared, slapping a hand on the table.

"There's more."

The brothers settled, faces like stone as Wrath continued. "We tracked them up to the outskirts of Sydney. Whatever was left of that city is gone, it's been taken over by slavers, cartel and bastards."

"Fuck," Pope bit out beside me. "Fucking fuck!"

"Boys in fatigues, men in militia all running the joint. Not sure if they were playing army or actually part of it at one point, either way we weren't getting in without an invitation."

"Found our women and kids, they were all in a pen together. Naked, shivering, hungry. Shit everywhere." Wrath ran a hand through his hair. "So, we blew up a bike as a distraction, stole a truck and drove it through the fence. Managed to get a few and get the fuck outta dodge. The brothers headed for the Plantation. I headed here."

"The rest?" Texas asked.

Wrath shrugged. "Maybe sold by now. Definitely moved. Either way, couldn't risk going back and getting captured. My duty was getting word to you."

Hazard cleared his throat. "I've read Shield's plan. He wants us to settle in, buckle down, fortify, make ourselves safe and do what we need to survive."

His lips twisted. "He also assumed we wouldn't have any more fuel."

"Yeah, met Whip on the road only a few hours outta town. He's gonna keep riding to the Plantation via Cunnamulla. Will inform Shield I made it, and relay the news about the massacres and meat market." Wrath shook his head. "No one will want to let this stand, but we're out gunned until we can get some of you up to Queensland."

"Get us up?" Chief asked.

"Guns," Hazard said, crossing his arms. "Shield's managed to get his hands on a cache of weapons that would make your mother cry."

Wrath nodded. "Got us a few contacts, men willing to exchange some information for food. The tips led us to a storehouse the local constabulary wasn't keeping too well staffed. Wasn't hard to persuade them to let us take a shopping trip."

There were grins around the table.

Wrath sobered. "We got shelter, we got weapons—though we'll need to move them down south. The real issues now are food and fuel. That's in Shield's plan as well."

Hazard leaned forward. "The Prez wants to turn us all into ranchers and truckers. Set up a pipeline, a sharing-bartering system."

No one moved but resignation crossed all their faces. We'd expected this. Had known it was coming for months. The life we'd lived before, whatever skills or shit we'd had, were useless. What mattered now was what skills could contribute to our survival. There was no going back.

Regret, bitterness, and resignation sat in my belly, a foul taste on my tongue. Perhaps I'd convinced myself that sometime in the future it would all come good again. But Shield's directive blew that fantasy away. This was our reality now.

"He expected us to need to use horses to transport it." Wrath laughed. "Turns out you got your own fuel station right here."

Yeah, we did. Thanks to Ellie.

"So, what now?" Pope asked.

All eyes went to Hazard. He leaned forward, his expression grim.

"In two weeks, we're sending a contingent up to Cunnamulla.

They'll replenish fuel in the safe houses along the way. At the Bunker, they'll set up another refinery. Then they'll move to the Plantation and do the same."

My gut clenched, knowing what was coming.

"Ellie and Runner will be in the contingent. She'll train a team here on how to produce the fuel over the next two weeks to keep it running while she's gone. Then she'll do the same for the other chapters."

The protest hovered on the tip of my tongue, anger sizzling through my veins. This was my woman they were putting in danger. *Mine.*

Hazard looked around. "Ghost, Texas and Pope will accompany. And I don't doubt the she-devil will want to ride along."

The table chuckled; Ava had already earned herself a formidable nickname.

"Wrath will act as guide, and you'll take Kate as well."

"Kate?" Wrath asked, eyebrows raising.

"You said the other chapters were struggling. We need someone who can teach them how to plant a fucking seed without it dying."

The table chuckled again.

"Besides, she's known, she understands how clubs work. She'll be able to smooth over any issues; a bridge of sorts."

"So, Ice'll be coming too?" Wrath clarified.

"Nope, his leg puts him out of commission for at least two months." Hazard nodded at Wrath. "She'll ride with you."

His mouth tightened but he nodded, accepting the responsibility.

Good luck, brother.

"We good?"

Nods.

166

CHAPTER TWENTY-FIVE

"Then dismissed."

Ghost opened the soundproof door, screams immediately assaulting our ears.

We pushed through the doorway, hands finding weapons as we rushed through the Club House and outside.

I stumbled to a halt, my weapon still in hand, heart in my motherfucking throat as I watched the women jump around, clutching each other, screeching like fucking banshees into the evening sky.

"Fuck, did someone feed them cocaine?" Pope asked, holstering his weapon.

Ellie spotted me, her grin splitting her face. "Audrey did it!" she squealed, racing over to grab my hand and pull me into the screeching mob.

In the middle sat the woman, her face flushed, her grin massive.

I crouched, Hazard and Pope doing the same as she held out a modified mobile phone to Hazard. Beside her, sat an open briefcase, electronics and a small collapsible antenna protruding from the inside.

"It's for you," she said, laughing.

Hazard hit loud speaker. "Who's this?"

"Only your worst nightmare motherfucker," Ava laughed, her voice clear and loud. A second later, "Danger Zone" by Kenny Loggins blasted down the line.

Hazard stared down at the phone for a beat then looked at Audrey. "Where is she?"

"On the other side of your lake!" She laughed, pointing. The lake stretched for miles.

"You made a telephone line?" Pope asked.

"Baby, I designed my own network," Audrey crowed, her

laugh joyful. "If my calculations are correct, this thing could stretch as far as two hundred miles, give or take depending on mountains, cities and other interruptions."

I saw Hazard's expression shift. "If I wanted to communicate with someone in say, Queensland, what would I need?"

Audrey laughed. "At least thirty of these little buggers planted between here and there to relay the signal." She pushed up to her feet, dusting off her butt. "You'd also need phones enabled with the A-frequency, a bunch of solar panels to keep the equipment charged, and a shit ton of lip balm."

"A-frequency?" Hazard asked.

"Audrey, motherfucker!"

"Lip balm?" Pope repeated, shooting me a confused glance.

"For all the lips that are gonna have to kiss my arse to get me to make that many devices." She cackled, slapping her arse, and turning away from us, moving to let Lottie pull her into a hug.

"Don't even think it," Pope warned Hazard, waggling a finger in his face. "I know how your mind works."

"It'd be a shit ton safer than having men riding up and down," Hazard replied with a shrug, pushing to his feet, and pocketing the phone.

"It'd delay us," I pointed out.

"Not if she only built enough for Cunnamulla, then assembled the rest when there and so on." Hazard shrugged. "Guess you better add one to your number boys, she's going with you."

Pope swore. "Why couldn't it have been the young one."

"Because you're not interested in Beth," I responded, rolling my eyes. "You just like how she sings."

Pope shrugged. "And how she blushes when I tease her. Reminds me of—" he snapped off, his lips pressing together, his body rigid. Grief flashed in his eyes before he smothered it, turning away.

I know brother. I'm sorry.

I clapped him on the shoulder. "Well, looks like she's riding with you."

"Over my fucking dead body!" He shoved me; the grief hidden once more.

"It's either her or the she-devil."

Pope eyed Ava. "I'd take her for a—"

Ghost slapped him over the head. "Ava rides with me."

"Well, fuck."

I chuckled, moving through the crowd, finding my girl. She chatted excitedly with Lottie and Zero. Lottie and her gesturing wildly and laughing freely, Zero simply watching Lottie.

I hid a smile, coming up to pull Ellie back into my chest.

"You good, baby?"

She nodded, her grin huge. "Isn't this wonderful? Audrey's a genius."

I nodded, my head dipping to nuzzle into her hair, my lips finding the shell of her ear. "Need to taste you, Baby Girl."

She immediately turned, raising up to kiss me, her lips parting sweetly as I tasted her. She tasted like perfection.

Chapter Twenty-Six

Runner

"So, we're going?" Ellie asked, her fingers tracing the tattoos on my chest.

"Mmhmm," I murmured, eyes closed enjoying the quiet. "As soon as Audrey has enough of her devices built."

"She said two weeks."

"Then that's when we leave." I opened one eye. "You worried?"

"No, just going to miss this." She waved a hand at the room. "And Blair."

I closed my eye, settling back. "Your sister will be safe here. And she's needed."

"I know." Ellie's hands continued to trace my tattoos, swirling and grazing, soft and sweet. "Are you looking forward to the ride?"

"Mm. Looking forward to hitting Cunnamulla."

"Oh?"

"Good club up there. Also, where I'm gonna ink your name on me."

Ellie's fingers stuttered to a halt. "What?"

I tapped my chest, above my heart. "Right here, Baby Girl. Hummer's the best tattooist in the club. He'll be doing it for me."

Water dotted my chest and I sighed, sitting up rolling over until Ellie was in my arms. "Baby Girl, you can't keep crying like this."

"I just love you so much." She twisted, hungrily kissing me, her hands fisting in my hair, pressing herself into me.

"Need you," she panted against my lips. "Please, Runner."

I was never gonna deny her a thing. If she'd ask, I'd cut out my fucking heart for her.

"On your back," I ordered. She rolled giving me a naughty grin as I loomed over her.

"You gonna suck my cock before I make you come" I asked, lazily stroking my cock. Her gaze dropped, her eyes flaring with hunger as she licked her lips and nodded.

Fuck.

I fed it to her, groaning as she sucked me deep. She gagged as I hit the back of her throat but whimpered, needing me so much that she pulls back before thrusting herself forward, her throat closing around me, hot, wet and oh so fucking perfect.

"Suck it," I barked, letting her work me. "Milk my cock, Baby Girl. You want my cum, baby? Fucking take it."

She groaned around my cock, her head and hands moving in tandem as she drove me higher, fucking my cock. I let her, knowing it worked her up, knowing she was getting off on my taste, on my words, on the way I couldn't stop the precum decorating her tongue.

"Fuck," I grunted, ripping myself back, dropping down and throwing her legs over her head. I held them with my shoulders, glaring down at her.

"Brace."

I thrust in, Ellie's scream breaking as I pulled back and lunged again, fucking her, brutally rough.

She *loved* it. Ellie broke under me, sobbing as she came, her tight snatch milking me violently as she found her release.

I thrust once, twice, then detonated, roaring my release, emptying myself into her, burying myself deep and finding heaven in her body.

Mine. Mine. Mine.

The chant continued long after our bodies had cooled and Ellie had drifted to sleep.

Mine. Mine Mine.

When we returned from our mission, I'd bring her back here. To this cabin on the lake, where we'd be safe from threats while I fucked her until her body was pliant and ready to accept my seed.

I'd fuck a baby into her.

Satisfaction warmed my chest. I couldn't give her a ring, but I could give her the kutte that I'd ordered the club's seamstress make.

I rolled, pulling my woman closer, knowing we needed to return to the compound. Eventually, we'd be missed and someone would come out to bring us home or Ellie's guilt would soon force us back and into work shifts.

But until then we'd stay here. In the honeymoon cabin, in this bed, wrapped in each other.

The before may have given me conveniences that made my life easier, but the after gave me Ellie. And I wouldn't trade her for the world.

"Runner?"

"Mm?"

CHAPTER TWENTY-SIX

"I know what I want."

"What?"

She grinned. "The favour you owe me. After I let you drug me."

"Ah." I pulled her in pressing a kiss to her shoulder. "Hit me."

She closed her eyes, giving me a sleepy smile, relaxing back into me. "Promise me that we'll always come here. Just the two of us."

Perfect for me.

I leaned down, pressing a kiss to her gorgeous lips, watching her smile sleepily, her eyes still closed.

"I promise, Baby Girl." I kissed her again. "Love you, Ellie."

Epilogue

Runner

The music vibrated through my chest, the beer in my hand was ice cold, and the food in my belly had tasted fucking ace. Ellie wore a dress she'd found somewhere, and my patch on her back. Every time I caught a glimpse of *Property of Runner* and her sexy arse in that fucking dress I got hard.

She'd let me fuck her while she wore only my claim last night. I'd carry that fucking memory to my grave.

We'd delayed leaving until Audrey had assembled a cache of her mobile network devices. She'd bitched and moaned the whole time, but I'd caught her hard at work in the early hours of the morning, a small grin on her face as she merged machinery together to create a lifeline we'd long thought gone.

We'd be leaving tomorrow.

The Canberra chapter had arrived and were settling in but there'd still been a few rough moments as we all found our new normal.

Doesn't help that their ex-President is a dick.

Glass kept getting in people's faces, demanding to be treated like a president even though he'd been given the distinction of a vice president when they amalgamated. Their previous VP having been downgraded to Enforcer, though the man had quietly thanked Hazard and admitted he was fucking glad not to be serving under Glass any more.

Red fucking flag.

Hazard had called for this send-off party knowing we needed to blow off steam.

I caught Ellie around the waist, pulling her close, swaying her in time to the music.

"Good, Baby Girl?" I asked, nuzzling her hair, knowing she'd be hotter than hell if I sucked on her earlobe.

"Perfect," she replied, twisting in my arms to wrap her arms around my neck. "Gonna miss this though."

"What? Camp outs?"

"Mm." She tilted her head towards the crowd. "The compound feels like home now." She gave a little shimmy, pressing her body against mine. "Maybe we could sneak off and—"

"Fuck you!"

The roar interrupted Ellie, and I sighed, recognizing the voice.

Glass.

"God," Ellie rolled her eyes. "What's his problem?"

Good question.

We followed the crowd, finding Hazard with his arms crossed, watching Glass pace in front of him, spewing obscenities, and slapping fists against his chest.

The music lowered, a crowd gathering.

"This piece of shit," Glass yelled, pointing at Hazard. "He's not man enough to run this fucking club."

Hazard's eyebrow lifted; a small sarcastic smile twisting his lips. "Let it out man, tell us how you really feel."

"Right here, right now, you and me. Winner gets the club," Glass yelled pointing at the dirt.

"And the loser?"

"Gets the fuck out."

Hazard tilted his head, looking over at Chief with a smile. "You cool with those terms?"

Chief shrugged. "Sounds fine to me."

Hazard shrugged off his kutte, folding it and holding it out to Blair who stood nearby. He hit her with a wink. "Hold that for me darlin.'"

She took it, looking from Glass to him. "You better win."

"Don't worry, I will."

Glass stepped up, holding his fists at the ready.

Chief stepped forward. "First down wins."

"Works for me," Hazard said with a shrug.

"Call it," Glass ordered.

Chief put his arm out in front of him, calling, "Three, two, one, go!" He threw his arm up and backed the hell up as Glass surged forward, throwing wild punches.

Hazard chuckled, easily ducking.

"He's good," Ellie murmured.

"He and Ghost served together. Some kind of special force super fucking secret government agency."

Ellie smiled at me then lifted her eyebrow. "Wait, you're not kidding?"

"Nope." I jerked my head at Ghost who stood in the shadows, watching Hazard as he began to demolish Glass, breaking him down, teaching him a lesson as he overpowered the cocky bastard. "Ghost was a lifer. He doesn't reveal much but it's enough to know he was recruited young. Like really fucking young. Only left when Hazard asked him to."

Ellie blinked. "And Hazard?"

I shrugged. "Got in, got out. Doesn't say much about it."

A yelp and thud ended the fight, Glass faceplanting, knocked out cold.

Hazard raised his arms, thumping his chest. "Next?" he yelled, looking around.

No one stepped forward.

"You're in my compound you play by my rules. Here, we're Nameless Souls. We live together, we ride together, we fucking *die* together. You can't deal with that, you get the fuck out, tonight."

Cheers and hollering followed his speech.

"Ride and die!" someone shouted.

"Ride and die!" the crowd yelled back.

Someone switched the music back on and the crowd began to disperse, prospects coming forward to drag Glass away.

Hazard found me in the crowd, gesturing me over.

"You sober?"

"Yeah."

"Can you organize the prospects to deal with this shit."

"On it."

Blair stepped forward, holding up Hazard's kutte. Blood streamed from a cut on his cheek, a lucky blow Glass had landed, his rings cutting the flesh.

"Come on," she said, shaking the kutte. "Put this on then we'll take care of that cut."

Hazard grinned at her; the expression almost feral. Heat and desire rampaged across his face. "You gonna kiss me better, Doc?"

She rolled her eyes. "It's me or Meat-Hand-McGee over

there." She nodded at Butcher. "You want a puckered scar marring your pretty face or you want a teeny line that will fade in less than a month?"

"Aww, Doc." He wrapped an arm around her neck, pulling her close. "Didn't know you'd looked that close."

She laughed, allowing him to draw her in but moving them both towards the infirmary. "Come on, President-No-Brains. Let's get you stitched up."

Ellie watched them, her expression curious.

"What?"

"I thought he was sweet on Ava."

"The she-devil?" I laughed. "Nah, was just sussing her out."

"What?"

I shook my head. "Never mind."

I then directed the prospects to dispose of Glass, stripping him of his possessions and everything that connected him to the Nameless Souls. Two of the prospects will drive him out, heading for the mountains in the distance. He'd be given the same send-off Gus had received. Whether he survived, would be up to him.

I found Ellie on the dance floor. She'd somehow persuaded Ava to join her. They moved in tandem, rubbing against each other as they danced, laughing as they swayed in a rhythm to the heavy, sexual song.

"Fuck," I muttered, leaning against the wall Ghost had been propping up all night. "That's my woman."

He didn't answer, but then I didn't expect him to but I couldn't help but niggle him a little.

"Don't like the she-devil but I get the attraction right now."

I grinned as Ghost shot me a sideways glare that said *fuck you.*

"You fucked her yet?"

His face tightened but it was enough to tell me he hadn't. And it was driving him fucking crazy.

"Long trip ahead of us, brother." I clapped him on the shoulder. "Plenty of time to get what you want."

I pushed away from the wall, leaving him in the shadows, a voyeur to Ava's enjoyment. He'd learn soon enough that to get what you wanted in the after, you had to take it.

And knowing that, I scooped Ellie up, throwing her over my shoulder just as I'd done that first night. She squealed, laughing as I headed towards our apartment.

"You right up there, Baby Girl?" I asked, my hand caressing her bottom.

She reached down, squeezing my arse, laughter coating every word as she answered, "There's nowhere I'd rather be."

Me either.

***

Thank you so much for reading Runner and Ellie's story! I loved writing this book and I hope you fell in love with them as much as I did.

I'm always looking for more people to join my ARC team. If you'd be interested, please fill out the form here.

Next up in this series is Wrath's story. You can get his book in Kindle Unlimited by clicking here.

Be sure to follow my Facebook page or check out my website for dates on when more books in this series are coming.

Next in Series

Wrath | Book 2 Nameless Souls MC

Kate

The forecourt of the compound bustled with activity. I watched, Switch and Zero, load the last of the gear into the back of a Wrangler. Off to one side, stood the rest of our traveling pack.

There was Ellie, our biochemist and the woman who'd created fuel from corn, and her man, Runner. They'd hooked up the night we'd arrived at the compound and had been joined at the hip ever since. Her fuel was the reason we were headed north, working our way up to the other Nameless Souls Motorcycle Club chapters'. We were going to teach them how to make their own biofuel.

Beside them crouched Audrey, her long black hair pulled back into a ponytail. She had an open case on the ground and was pointing at the electronics inside. Pope stood over her, arms crossed as he made some comment that had her rolling her eyes. Audrey had designed her own mobile network which she was calling the 'A-Network'. The cases held the transmitters that would relay the signals from her readjusted mobile phones. If it worked, and it would because Audrey knew her shit, it would be the first type of communications between cities we'd had since the before.

Beyond them, Jo, our mechanic, and Texas stood in front

of the two fuel tankers, playing scissors, paper, rock. Ava, our security specialist, and Ghost, the club's Sergeant at Arms, examined the retrofitted plating on the tankers, checking for weaknesses. Butcher and Lottie, the club's doctor, and our resident vet, rounded out our party.

Except for Wrath.

I glanced around, trying to be subtle as I looked for the nomad biker.

Runner raised two fingers to his mouth letting out an ear-splitting whistle. I grimaced but moved closer. From a building on the far right, Wrath emerged, a bag slung over one shoulder, a brown bag in his other hand. I recognised his loose-hipped, confident walk. The way his head moved slightly every now and then, as if he were constantly scoping his surrounds, searching for danger.

My heart gave a weird skip, an ache taking up residence somewhere in my middle.

"We ready?" Runner asked, looking at the assembled group.

"Bikes are loaded, trailer's good." Switch reported.

"Tankers are ready," Jo replied, flicking her braid over her shoulder. "Though not sure your boy's up to the challenge of driving the big rig."

"Baby," Texas drawled, crossing his arms, and giving her a cocky grin. "I know exactly how to handle a big rig."

Runner ignored him, looking to Audrey.

"The comms are loaded and I've plotted the locations where we'll need to offload them. The real issue will be putting them in secure locations."

"We'll deal with that when we get there," Pope said, running a hand through his hair. "The real issue will be hiding the fuel in the safe houses."

"Nope," Wrath commented coming up to the group. He reached across handing me the paper bag and shrugging off the backpack. "The real issue will be keeping out of reach of militia, cults, and bastards."

The pandemic had come a few years ago, rapidly spreading across the world and forcing border closures and shutting down supply lines. At first, it had looked like we'd overcome it, that it would be a short thing. But then the vaccine had arrived and caused an unexpected result – it'd mutated the disease.

When the world had finally ended, it hadn't been with a bang. Instead, it'd happened with a whimper. Trust had eroded over years as food become scarce and people died. When the government hadn't been able to deliver on basic promises – like a vaccine – society had reverted to violence to survive. When the world finally went dark – the power grid going down, the communications falling silent, it had been an end to a long, painful death.

And yet here we were. Alive. Surviving in the after.

I'd holed up in my University, just me and twelve other women. We'd survived, using our skills to thrive. I was a qualified botanist, and had been completing my doctorate focusing on nanoparticle use to increase crop stress tolerance and yield.

I guess that was now over.

I hadn't planned on ever returning to the Nameless Souls MC. Gus, my father, had been a monster, and when I'd finally escaped, I'd made it so he wouldn't find me. Returning had been a nightmare, but I'd done it when The Purge, a rogue cult group that enslaved women, had overrun the College, injuring Ava, and putting us all at risk.

We'd survived that invasion but knew more were on the way.

We'd needed help, more protection, so I'd brought them here – to the compound. Throwing myself on my father's mercy had been a deeply shameful humbling experience. But I'd done it, and in return, he'd tried to drug Ellie and sell her into slavery.

He'd been punished for his actions but it didn't stop me from feeling shame. My own blood had tried to harm a woman I deeply respected and loved like a sister.

"Bastards?" Jo asked, drawing my attention back to the group.

Wrath reached out, tapping the brown bag still clutched in my hand. "Eat."

He looked back at Ava. "Bastards, mutated humans."

"Mutated how?" Lottie asked.

He shrugged. "Some are crazy. The virus having corrupted their mind. They're more animal than human but pathetic, easily overpowered. Others are strong, vicious, smart. But their overwhelming desire is to kill or fuck."

"Wait. Wait, wait, wait. Wait a damned second," Audrey said, holding up a hand. "Are you saying there are goddamned zombies out there?"

"No, these beasts aren't dead. They're just corrupted."

A quick glance around the group revealed that only us women were surprised by this news.

"You've seen them?" I asked Wrath. It was my first question to him in over five years. My first words to him since… I pushed the memory away.

He looked at me, his dark eyes staring, questioning, evaluating. Finally, he nodded.

"I've killed them."

Books by Evie Mitchell

Nameless Souls MC Series
Runner
Wrath
Ghost

Elliot Security Series
Rough Edge
Bleeding Edge
Knife Edge

Capricorn Cove Series
Thunder Thighs
Double the D
Muffin Top
The Mrs. Clause
Beach Party
New Year Knew You
The Shake-Up
Double Breasted
As You Wish
You Sleigh Me
Resolution Revolution
Meat Load
Trunk Junk

Archer Sibling Series
Just Joshing

Thor's Shipbuilding Series
Clean Sweep
The X-List
Reality Check
The Christmas Contract

Other Books
Reign
Puppy Love

CPSIA information can be obtained
at www.ICGtesting.com
Printed in the USA
FSHW022345100222
88208FS